MONEY TO BURN

MONEY TO BURN

BY E. M. GOLDMAN

VIKING

Thanks to David Foss, R.C.M.P. (Ret.)
—E.M.G.

VIKING
Published by the Penguin Group
Penguin Books USA Inc., 375 Hudson Street, New York, New York 10014, U.S.A.
Penguin Books Ltd, 27 Wrights Lane, London W8 5TZ, England
Penguin Books Australia Ltd, Ringwood, Victoria, Australia
Penguin Books Canada Ltd, 10 Alcorn Avenue, Toronto, Ontario, Canada M4V 3B2
Penguin Books (N.Z.) Ltd, 182–190 Wairau Road, Auckland 10, New Zealand

Penguin Books Ltd, Registered Offices: Harmondsworth, Middlesex, England

First published in 1994 by Viking, a division of Penguin Books USA Inc.

1   3   5   7   9   10   8   6   4   2

Library of Congress Cataloging-in-Publication Data

Goldman, E. M.
Money to burn / by E. M. Goldman.   p.   cm.
Summary: Two teenage boys are torn between opportunity and danger
when they stumble upon $400,000 in drug money.
I S B N   0 - 6 7 0 - 8 5 3 3 9 - 9
[1. Money—Fiction.   2. Friendship—Fiction.]   I. Title.
PZ7.G56795Mo   1994   [Fic]—dc20   93-14584   CIP   AC

Printed in U.S.A.   Set in Bembo

TO THE EXTER MOB:

ALICE

SIM

INEKE

ANNA

MAX

MONEY TO BURN

CHAPTER
1

MONEY.

Matt wanted some. He was fourteen, and it was summer and hot, and he and Lewis were both broke.

"Money." Matt sighed.

Lewis looked around, his dark hair flopping over until it almost hit the top of his glasses. "Money? Where?"

"Nowhere." That was the problem.

Messing around on their bikes provided the only excitement that they were likely to find in Potts. Except for a few narrow rocky beaches along the ocean, the town didn't have much to offer if you were broke.

School had been out for a week. Every day they had packed their towels and biked the short stretch of tree-lined highway to Joneson Park, located in Upper Potts. (The older part of town, where he and Lewis both lived and where the pulp mill was located, was just plain Potts.)

"Too crowded," Lewis said when they stopped their bikes near the wharf and looked down toward the beach. "Too many people fighting it out for every grain of sand."

If so, most had died in combat. Bodies lay everywhere, glistening in the sun. Some of those bodies were truly grim to behold, dough-colored and puffy. Others glowed neon red, as though they had been dunked in sweet-and-sour sauce mixed with radioactive waste. No one moved except to slather on more suntan lotion.

Even though it was only eleven o'clock, the pavement already threatened to blister Matt's feet through his running shoes. Both boys kept their feet moving while they stood straddling their bikes. "Too many little kids." Little kids threw sand, and every other minute one fell down and cried.

Too bad he and Lewis didn't have more quarters for the arcade attached to the bowling alley. Too bad the arcade hadn't gotten any new games since last February. Too bad it wasn't likely to get any before next February.

They stayed near the wharf, making lazy circles on their bikes. They rode so slowly that they kept swerving to avoid running into each other. Every now and then Lewis hit a pothole, and then he'd swear and have to get off.

Matt had a mountain bike since his birthday in March. He had absolute faith that his Trailblazer wouldn't dump him, not if he rode up Mount Everest or down through a moon crater. It didn't dump him now, but he could feel through his legs how much it hated going slow.

Later, he promised.

Later, when he was alone, he'd take his Trailblazer and they'd burn up one of the side paths. Right now he was with Lewis, who was stuck riding a three-gear girl's bike that his mom bragged she found dirt-cheap at a garage sale. Lewis' bike was better than nothing, but not much.

Before they rode off with no destination in mind, Matt looked back again toward the beach. There were lots of little kids, all right. Lots of big sisters watching them, too. Matt didn't mention to his friend how easy it was to talk to a girl who was truly bored with brushing sand off a baby's bottom and locating its plastic shovel. Lewis was intelligent enough that he'd skipped a grade, meaning he was almost a year younger than Matt. He hadn't discovered big sisters yet.

These days, Matt seemed to be discovering them all the time.

Money. He supposed that when he got around to choosing a girlfriend, he'd have to get some for movies and things.

As they headed toward the main street and the stores, Matt slowed automatically so Lewis could keep up. "We could try Wong's Market," he suggested when they stopped on the street to consider whether they wanted to buy Slurpees. "Wong's has definite possibilities."

Lewis shook his head, then pushed back his hair with an impatient gesture. "I'm not buying a Slurpee there. Not unless Wong has fixed his machine."

The Slurpee machine at Wong's had two flavors, cream soda and raspberry. Both had the consistency of spit and the sickening sweet taste of a fluoride treatment. The main difference was that the cream soda was almost see-through. Raspberry Slurpees had that shade of angry pink Matt associated with picking off a scab too soon. "We could ask him for jobs, I mean."

One of Lewis' eyebrows disappeared into his hair. "I think you have to be Chinese to work for Wong."

"I'll be Chinese." He steadied his bike between his knees so he could put a finger at each side of his eyes to stretch them out. He grinned at Lewis. "How's that?"

"Aw, man. Of course you'll have to explain why you're walking around that way." Lewis looked thoughtful. "It might work if you dye your hair black. I can probably borrow some of that Clairol stuff my mom uses."

Matt was blond. His hair would be almost white by summer's end. "Sounds good." He knew what Lewis was doing. This time he wouldn't be the one to laugh first.

"The problem is that your eyes are blue. You won't be able to look at him straight on." One corner of Lewis's mouth twitched.

"I'll wear my sunglasses." He thought of sad things. Lewis's bike.

A snort escaped from the other boy. "Naw, it wouldn't work. Wong would probably say something to you in Chinese."

"I speak Chinese. Hey, *moo goo gai pan*. I think that means Happy New Year." Which ought to be really easy to work into the conversation in July. "I'll do it if you will."

"Wong tossed me out last week for reading his books without buying anything. He'd recognize me." Lewis blinked as if the conversation had abruptly turned serious. "He'd recognize these." He touched the black tape holding his glasses together. "Besides, everybody who works at the market is a relative of his."

"Maybe you can get him to adopt you."

"Maybe."

Matt was the first to spot the blue-and-white patrol car heading in their direction. A few seconds later, the car whooshed past them. He prepared to wave, then let his hand fall when he saw that the police officer wasn't Daisy, the lady Jack was dating. Jack was Matt's father, who ran a café near the mill.

"Something might be happening," Lewis said,

turning his bike around. Matt got ready to ride off, too. Potts had never had a shoot-out. This would be a really good day for one.

The car turned the corner, then stopped at the post office. The policeman got out with envelopes in his hand.

Neither boy moved. "Crap," Lewis said. "No excitement there."

No such luck.

A few days earlier, the police and the ambulance had gone to Joneson Park when a man collapsed near the entrance to the beach trail. Matt and Lewis weren't there, but a friend saw everything. He said the guy wasn't really old, although he wasn't young either. Built like Santa Claus. Wearing a brown suit. The first anybody noticed him was when he started staggering around with his hand on his chest. Then he fell. Somebody tried CPR, but he died anyway.

Matt knew a lot of older people in town from hanging around the café. He felt relieved when he found out this wasn't one of them. The dead man had been passing through town, alone. The police were still trying to locate his family.

Nothing interesting had happened in Potts since then.

"A SMALL SLURPEE, please," Lewis called as they went inside the little market. Wong sat behind the counter, which had lottery results posted everywhere and base-ball cards under plastic sheeting. A small fan was on a second wooden chair next to him, shifting around warm air.

"Medium for me." They put down their money.

Lewis looked through a box of wooden animal fig-ures on sticks while they waited for Wong to hand over the paper cups. He picked up a carved monkey with arms that flung open when he pulled a string at the back. "How much is this?"

The middle-aged man told him.

Lewis replaced the toy slowly, then turned to take his cup. "Joey's still too little, anyway," he said to Matt. Lewis's nephew was seven months old.

"New flavor," Wong said, nodding toward the ma-chine, which was past the wicker baskets and souvenir T-shirts. "Cola."

Matt gave the man a big smile, the kind that, when he was younger, used to make his father's female customers offer to adopt him. "Thanks. We'll try that."

Their choices were raspberry and cola. They both opted for cola. After the machine dribbled sluggishly into their cups, they examined what was inside. "It looks like his dog was sick," Lewis said under his breath.

Matt stuck in his straw. "Tastes like his dog was sick, too."

Lewis tried some. "Maybe this *is* his dog." He smacked his lips. "Yum. Schnauzer."

If so, Wong had added lots of sugar to try to disguise the fact. "Let's ask him about jobs," Matt said. Lewis hung back. "Hey, what's the worst that can happen?"

"No work," Mr. Wong said. He was fanning himself with a copy of *Sports Illustrated*. "No work here."

Matt and Lewis exchanged glances. Matt swallowed. "We'd really like to work for you," he said. "I've helped out at my dad's café. See, that way you'll get two of us for the price of one. Lewis can sweep while I sit up front." He caught Lewis' startled glance. "We'd trade around, of course. Hey, Mr. Wong, if you had people working for you, maybe you could get outside yourself. You could go swimming, stuff like that."

Matt had never passed the market without seeing Wong there. The store opened early, too. He figured that Wong had to be setting out the morning newspapers at about the same time that the café began preparing for the breakfast crowd, which was mostly single guys working at the mill. The market hours were posted on the door, so Matt knew that it didn't close until midnight.

"Swimming." Wong drew out the word.

For a second Matt thought the man was considering

hiring them. Then Wong turned and called out something in Chinese.

A soft voice answered behind the flowered curtain separating the main area of the store from the back. A girl with long black hair came out. Slightly older than he was, Matt guessed. Fifteen or so. She wore a brown apron over a lime green T-shirt and jeans. She said something to Mr. Wong, ducking a little as she spoke, then gazed shyly at the two boys.

"This is my wife's niece," Mr. Wong said. "She is working in the store. *She* . . ." He said something else Matt didn't understand. The only word he did understand was "swimming." The girl looked puzzled.

"Maybe," Matt said, "maybe we could work here sometimes, and then you could both go swimming." Sure, and Wong's wife could go swimming and his old mother could dive off the rocks. His voice trailed off. "Or maybe not."

He wondered whether the girl spoke English at all. "Hi," he said. "Me—Matt." He pointed toward Lewis. "Him—Lewis." He pointed at her. "You—" He waited.

"Sara Lee," she said with no accent at all. "Hi."

"Sara Lee," Lewis blurted out. "That's a kind of—" He stopped, maybe because Matt elbowed him. Sara Lee was a type of really good cheesecake.

Matt felt glad that his cheeks were sunburned. "I didn't think you spoke English."

9

"Actually," she said, "it's my Chinese that's rusty." Mr. Wong said something to her. "My uncle says he wishes you luck in finding employment."

"Thanks," Matt said. "We'll need it." They both started toward the open door with their Slurpees. Matt stopped so quickly that Lewis almost ran into him. "Are you going to be here all summer?" he asked her.

She had started to straighten a display of candy bars, but she turned and nodded. "Until school starts in September. Sorry to disappoint you."

"No disappointment." Matt cleared his throat. "Maybe I'll see you around."

"Maybe."

"MAYBE I'LL SEE you around," Lewis mimicked as they returned to where they had left their bikes, beneath the maple tree in front of the art gallery. He always packed a paperback book, usually a fantasy with a cover that showed armor-clad warriors or magicians in bathrobes. For a second he stood looking into his bike pack like he was debating taking out his book and reading while they drank. He didn't.

Matt wore shorts, Lewis cut-offs. They sat on yellowing grass that felt like a stiff hairbrush, both of them keeping their backs to the tree and their knees up so their bare legs wouldn't be prickled.

"I was being friendly." Matt stirred his Slurpee, which looked less sickening now that it had given up any pretense of being frozen. "After all, she's new here and she's—"

"What? Chinese?"

She wasn't, not any more than Matt was Swedish or English.

"She's short." The top of the girl's head didn't even reach his shoulder. Her hair was down to her waist, too, and that fascinated him. Chances were that some mathematical formula covered the situation, like the one where you could find the height of a structure by measuring its shadow. Maybe you could also figure out things about a girl from the length of her hair.

Lewis nodded. "Right. She's short."

"Hey," Matt said. "I thought you munchkins stuck together."

Lewis didn't say anything and Matt was sorry he had.

The year before, he and Lewis had been pretty much the same height. Now Matt was a lot taller, with arms and legs that were beginning to feel like he'd borrowed them from a basketball player. A couple of times lately when he came into the café, he had knocked into tables. His father assured him that everything would fit together, sooner or later.

Probably he and Lewis would, too.

Right now they had an entire summer to fill. "Playland's open," Matt said. Playland was an amusement park in the city that was only open during the summer.

The rides were expensive. He sighed. "We need jobs."

"We need money."

They tossed around a few more ideas for raising cash. Matt and Lewis had both put in their names to cover newspaper routes for kids on vacation. Unfortunately, everybody else their age had the same idea.

Both would be willing to watch kids, but too many people only hired girls as sitters. Lewis even had experience with babies. His married sister had moved back home shortly after her son was born, so half of Lewis' room was taken up by Joey's crib. The other half was crammed with Joey's stuff. Lewis knew how to change diapers and everything. From the way he talked, a dead body would be a rose garden in comparison to some diapers.

In the past, Matt had worked sometimes for his father as a dishwasher. Dishwashers tended to leave as soon as they found better-paying work. This year's dishwasher was a retarded man Jack swore was the most careful worker he ever had. Ron really enjoyed working at the café. He showed no sign of pushing off.

"We could rob a bank," Matt suggested.

Lewis thought about that one for a while, like Matt knew he would. Jack said Lewis reminded him of a puppy trying out its teeth. He'd chew on anything. "We might have trouble getting away on our bikes."

Matt knew *he* wouldn't. "Oh. Right."

They drank in silence for a while longer. "We could look for bottles to cash in," Lewis said.

They could do that, all right. They probably would.

Matt looked at his watch. "It's almost noon." That meant the arcade was open. If Lewis had any quarters left, they could cycle up Blackberry Hill to the arcade.

Lewis didn't say anything, which Matt took to mean that he had spent his last quarters on the Slurpee. He should have known. If Lewis had any money, he would have bought the carved monkey.

Matt looked around at a day that seemed to have grown hotter and brighter outside the dappled shade thrown by the tree. No breeze stirred to ruffle the leaves. Down the street, the red and white maple leaf flag hung limply outside the post office. "We have to do something."

Lewis rested his head on his knees, letting his hands trail onto the grass. "Why?"

"It's summer." Suppose in September they had to write a paper on what they did during their vacation. At this rate, Matt would end up with a one-word essay.

Nothing.

It seemed like all the rest of their friends were going on vacation—camping, if nothing else. Jack always maintained that he couldn't leave the café. Lewis' family never went anywhere because his dad was a logger who did a little fishing whenever he got laid off. So far this year he hadn't found a fishing boat captain willing to hire him. He would, though. Lewis said he always did.

Matt yawned. They could cycle back to the café. Jack would give them lunch. He let them hang around as long as they wanted, with the understanding they had to vacate their table if a regatta of campers suddenly pulled in and decided they were tired of roughing it. (This had happened exactly once, but Jack still talked about it.)

They could head back to Matt's house to use his Nintendo. Jack only served breakfast and lunch at the Come Back Café, closing at three each day. That meant they'd have a couple of hours to watch videos before he came home and scolded them for being inside on a nice day.

They'd already seen everything on Matt's tapes.

By unspoken agreement, they didn't even consider going to Lewis' place.

It seemed unfair. Matt felt like he spent his whole school year stretching toward three-day weekends and the Christmas holidays and spring break. Summer arrived promising a fizz of excitement. This year's fizz was already going flat.

When they stood up, both scanned the community bulletin board, filled with various types of notices that people put up about lost pets and stoves for sale and meetings. Although somebody was advertising for twenty people who wanted to lose weight, nobody wanted to hire any boys.

"Old Dermot's put up a new poem." Lewis tapped a loose sheet of paper. "This one is kind of funny. About a seagull trying to decide what kind of garbage it wants for lunch. Like it's at a fancy restaurant."

Matt wasn't interested in poetry, but he looked. "Pretty good," he agreed just to be agreeable.

Dermot the Hermit was a sometime-beachcomber and sometime-fisherman who sometimes came into the café. Nobody wanted to publish his poems, so he'd gotten into the habit of hanging them on the bulletin board until the next strong wind blew them away.

"Do you want to go back to your place and play Nintendo?" Lewis asked.

"Sure." Both chucked their Slurpee cups into the garbage can outside the fish-and-chip shop.

"Let's go along the beach path," Matt suggested. "It's cooler." The faster way was a twenty-minute ride over the winding stretch of highway that passed the turnoff to the dump. If they went that way, they'd be traveling in direct sunlight. The beach path was longer, but it went through a thick, protected stand of big trees and ferns, ending at the Potts golf course.

"Good idea," Lewis agreed.

To get to the beach trail, they had to go through Joneson Park. They passed the place where the man had died of a heart attack a few days before, then went past the barricade that warned against taking motor-bikes beyond that point.

The temperature dipped about ten degrees as they entered the dark narrow path. At the same time, all sound ceased from the park, swallowed up by the giant trees and thick growth. Lewis sighed. "This is better."

It was also less smooth. The trail was uneven, with patches of thick mud remaining from the last rain. At some spots they had to lift their bikes over fallen limbs or walk around logs. But it was green and cool, and they didn't pass many people. They could see the ocean sparkling through the trees to their left. The foliage kept any noises from the highway away from them so it felt like they were miles from any other people. It was pleasant, at least until they reached a spot with a stagnant pool that had to be the home of a million mosquitoes.

Hungry mosquitoes.

Giant-sized, slavering, red-eyed mosquitoes that had been waiting in ambush for days.

Mosquitoes from another planet waiting to taste their succulent flesh before deciding whether to take over Earth.

"Crap."

They couldn't swat and steer their bikes around potholes at the same time. Matt hurried on as fast as he could until he reached a more even area of the path, then looked back when he heard a crash. "Are you okay?" he called.

"I got on my bike too soon," the other boy grumbled as he stood. "These stupid tires are almost bald." Matt rested his bike against the tree while his friend brushed himself off. They seemed to have passed the worst of the cloud of bloodsuckers. Lewis gestured toward a thick patch of ferns. "Go see what I hit, okay? There's something lying just off the path."

Matt found the object immediately, although he wouldn't have if he hadn't been looking. Something dark brown and flat-looking lay on one side of the path, concealed by ferns and blending in with the mud. Almost invisible. Maybe a cardboard box that had been soaked through by the last rain. He bent over to examine it. "Somebody threw away an old suitcase." He hated people littering places like the beach trail. Maybe he'd carry it out and dump it in one of the trash containers near the trail exit.

The bag was hard-cased, dirty, and scuffed as if it had been dragged. A deep scratch went all the way across one side. He reached for the gritty handle and picked it up. On the moist ground where the suitcase had been, long pink worms wriggled and sow bugs skittered away in every direction.

"It's heavier than it looks." Water had probably gotten in.

Lewis joined him. "Can you open it?"

"I can try." Matt used the bottom of his shirt to wipe off the clasps. He half expected the case to stick because of all the grit, but it popped right open.

What he saw made him sit down hard in the mud.

Lewis made a strangling noise and took a step backward.

The suitcase wasn't empty, not at all.

It was filled with money.

Lots of it.

CHAPTER
2

MATT HAD SEEN SUITCASES FULL OF MONEY BEFORE.

On TV.

Somebody always got hurt or killed carrying around suitcases full of money.

On TV.

A roaring sound like an avalanche filled Matt's head as he sat there with his bottom in the mud, and then things became absolutely still. "Lew? It's money."

"It can't be real." The light was thin, filtered through the trees, but Lewis was blinking like he was staring into the sun. "It's not, is it?"

Maybe Lewis had never seen a hundred-dollar bill up close. Matt had. After payday at the mill, hundreds often showed up at the café. "It sure looks real." Matt picked up one of the top stacks, held together with a paper band. Another stack lay below, and another stack of hundreds below that when he picked it up to see how deep they went. Some of the cash on the bottom was damp, and the paper bands fell apart as soon as he touched them.

Matt's skin prickled worse than when he had

chicken pox. The feeling became familiar. He leaped to his feet and swiped at himself with both hands. "The mosquitoes are eating me alive!"

They were chewing Lewis, too, but his friend didn't move from where he was hunkered down next to the suitcase. Behind his glasses, Lewis' eyes were so big, they looked like they had the time the eye doctor put in drops. He slapped a mosquito on his neck. "I can't even pinch myself to see if I'm dreaming."

Somewhere nearby a dog barked. Matt hurriedly closed the suitcase. "Maybe this is a dream, and maybe this isn't a dream. Either way, we have to get out of here." He paused. "Lew?"

Lewis took off his glasses, wiped them on his T-shirt, put them back on, and looked at the suitcase again. He straightened slowly. "Where did it come from?"

"We said we needed money, right? We've been good. Maybe it was Santa Claus." A joke. That's how he meant it.

Lewis shivered. "Nobody's been that good."

"I don't know how it got here." Matt picked up the case again, hefting it appreciatively. "This weighs as much as a bowling ball. That's a whole lot of hundred-dollar bills."

"Wet," Lewis said as though he was discussing a science project. "The suitcase is wet. Water weighs a lot."

Trust Lewis to argue at a time like this. They seldom had enough money to *count,* much less weigh. "Lewis, this is a whole lot of money."

Lewis just stood there.

Matt had seen Lewis the one time he was truly freaked, when his father had hit him and broken his glasses. At least that time Lewis was alive. He was angry and upset, but he was definitely all there. This was more like a coma.

"Lew," he said urgently, "we have to figure out what to do."

Nothing.

He was used to them making decisions together. Usually he'd say something and Lewis would either embellish his idea or shoot it down in flames. Sometimes Lewis made a suggestion, and then Matt had to wait until Lewis finished arguing with himself. This was big, and Lewis wasn't saying anything.

That was okay, Matt decided. He could take charge. He was older and bigger. "We're going to take it out of here."

Matt looked at his mountain bike, which was built really well for carrying him. He looked at Lewis' bike. That was when he discovered something good about a garage-sale bike that sure wasn't built for speed.

Sometimes you wanted a racehorse.

Sometimes you wanted a burro.

Lewis' bike had a rack.

Matt could not, *not* believe how long it took Lewis to find the bungee cord in his pack, plus a folded garbage bag. Then Lewis dropped the cord into the mud and had to pick it up again, and his fingers seemed unable to close on it. It was Matt who decided they should put the suitcase inside the bag because it was dirty and wet and because somebody might wonder about it. Neither of them seemed too steady as they attached the plastic-wrapped suitcase to the back of the bike.

Matt grabbed his bike from where it was leaning against a tree. "Come on, let's go." He waited. "Lew, *come on!*"

"Wait. I almost forgot the bottles." Lewis nodded toward a six-pack of empties lying under a bush. "That's what I was looking at when I fell down."

Beer bottles? At a time like this? "Hey, you don't need to cash in any bottles."

"Maybe you don't." Lewis opened up the garbage bag and put the empties on top of the suitcase full of money. "This is a great spot," he said before they pushed off. "We should come this way more often."

THERE WAS NO question of Lewis riding on the uneven trail, so Matt walked the Trailblazer a short distance behind him. The path was easy, with just a few trees to walk around. Even so, Lewis stumbled twice and

almost went down from the awkward weight. "Easy,"
Matt soothed him. "Take it easy."

They were taking their money for an easy walk
home.

At least, he thought of the money as theirs. Technically, he supposed the money belonged to Lewis because he was the one who had found it. Still, Lewis
was bound to share. They were friends, and Matt always shared with him. Matt had given Lewis his old
bike, only it caused problems when Lewis' dad yelled
at him for taking charity. Lewis had only had the bike
three days before his father ran over it with his truck
late at night. Lewis accused him to his face of wrecking
the bike deliberately. That was when Mr. Rannulf
hit him.

Now Lewis could buy a really good bike. And
glasses. And he'd never run out of quarters again in
his entire life.

WHEN THEY FINALLY emerged from the beach trail, the
direct sunlight was blinding. Both boys stood there,
looking out at a golf course which seemed an unnatural
shade of green. Beyond that, the mill puffed out lazy
plumes of steam, and beyond that, the sea was on fire.
Next to Matt, Lewis shivered as though they were
entering the shadows instead of leaving them. Everything felt different, like the brightness control had been

boosted on his TV. Even the air tasted different. Something had been added to the tang of summer and salt from the ocean.

"I'm hungry," Lewis said abruptly. "I'm really hungry."

So was Matt, although he hadn't realized it until then. He didn't know when he'd felt more hungry. He was ravenous for a tall order of pancakes with bacon on the side, plus a vanilla milkshake. For starters.

Maybe that was what money did to you. It got you starved for all kinds of things. "We'll head over to the café and fuel up," he said. After that, they'd go to Matt's house to count the money. Then they'd decide how to spend it.

By shading his eyes, Matt could just make out a few sailboats floating in the bay. "I want a boat," he announced. If he had his own boat, they wouldn't have to wait for a ferry every time they wanted to go into Vancouver. A red sports car would be good, too, except that he wasn't old enough to drive.

He liked the little golf carts with their flouncy tops. Maybe he wouldn't need a driver's license for one of them.

He didn't like the way the golfers kept glancing in their direction. When he said so, Lewis laughed in a way that wasn't really a laugh. "Can you imagine how we'd feel if we were actually planning to keep this money?"

24

Matt's little golf cart crashed into a tree. "Say again?"

Lewis was moving away. "I'll be glad when we hand the money over to your dad. This whole thing is making me sweat."

Matt's red sports car hurled itself off a cliff and exploded in flames. His boat sank.

"All I can say is there better be a reward."

Nonononononononononononononononononono.

Not a dream. This was a nightmare.

Honesty wasn't anything they had ever talked about. It wasn't like Lewis went to church or anything. Lewis' brother-in-law was in jail because he'd tried to rob a convenience store of cash and a package of Pampers. This wasn't at all the same thing. They had found this money. Lewis had found it.

Please, God, a joke. This had to be a joke.

Lewis was looking at him peculiarly. "You weren't thinking of keeping it, were you?"

Matt pinched himself, hard. He never even cheated on tests. Well, maybe once or twice, but not usually. He was almost positive that before school ended, one girl had tried to show him her paper during a test. She made really good grades. Not looking should count for something. He deserved that money. Lewis deserved it.

"Earth to Matt," Lewis said. "Come in, Matt."

Matt could see it. The local paper would run an ad

asking whether somebody had lost a suitcase full of money. Some guy with a yacht would turn up and give them each a five-dollar reward.

"What if nobody claims it?" What if people weren't standing in line?

Sure, I lost a suitcase full of money. Guess I was a little careless, ha, ha.

"Somebody will." They were up to the road now. "You know what I think?" Lewis said. "I think some old lady withdrew her life savings from the bank."

"Then she went for a walk and forgot that she was carrying all that money?"

Lewis' idea wasn't that far-fetched. Lots of retired people lived in Potts, some of them in nursing homes. Every now and then one wandered off. Most were found sooner or later, in one condition or other. Maybe one of them had decided to withdraw all her savings and then either got found or died.

Matt wished Lewis hadn't mentioned a little old lady. His reward had just dropped to a shiny dime.

They walked along in silence. After the green of the beach path and the gold sheen of the outside world, now Matt was seeing everything through a blood-red haze. He was choked.

"Are you mad?" Lewis asked when they reached the road.

"Mad?" Matt yelled. "Why should I be *mad?* Why do you think I'm *mad?"*

Lewis just stood there. "Sorry." He seemed almost ashamed. "If there's a reward, I'll split it with you."

Matt was about to yell some more when he realized something. Lewis was the one who didn't have anything. Lewis couldn't even afford a wooden toy for his nephew. In fact, now that Matt thought about it, Lewis was the one with the right to be mad. If you needed money, there had to be something truly unfair about finding money that your conscience wouldn't let you keep.

"I'm mad," Matt said gruffly, "but I'll get over it."

MAYBE HONESTY WAS the best policy, but as they walked into the busy café, Lewis looked green under his mosquito bites. Matt's heart was hammering so loudly in his ears that he could hardly hear.

He spotted Jack right away, pouring coffee for some customers in the corner. When his dad saw them, he raised a hand in greeting and indicated an empty booth near the door.

A booth was good. Lewis shoved the suitcase under the table, still in its plastic bag, and sat down. "We turn it in now, right?" Lewis sounded hopeful.

Matt groaned. *No way. We get out of here. We spend the cash.* That's what he wanted to say. "I guess so."

He went up to the counter to wait for his father. Jack looked really busy, so he didn't want to interrupt him. Also, he was in no hurry to stop being a millionaire. (Okay, a quarter of a millionaire. Lewis had estimated that the suitcase held at least $400,000.)

An elderly man was sitting at a nearby table. "Drugs," he said loudly to people at another table. Matt turned around. The man had a rolled-up copy of the local paper, the *Potts Gazette,* and was shaking it for emphasis. "Everywhere you look. Not just the city. Here. What next?" He waited. "Drugs for children. Young children. Children like this boy."

Matt wasn't sure that he liked being pointed out as a young child. "Nobody's ever tried to sell me any drugs," he said politely to the man.

Jack had come back to stand behind the counter. "These boys are too intelligent to get involved with anything like drugs."

End of subject. Matt took a deep breath. "Dad, can I talk with you a minute?"

"Sure." Jack frowned. "Just as long as you're not asking for a raise in your allowance."

"It's not that." Matt looked around.

"Secret stuff, huh?"

"More coffee, please, Jack," a man called.

"Coming right up!" He picked up a full coffeepot. "Look, son, Edith is at a doctor's appointment, so right now I'm swamped." Edith was a waitress. "You boys figure out what you want for lunch. Leave some food for my paying customers. Wait until the traffic clears, and then we'll talk."

Matt reported back to Lewis in the booth. "Maybe we should eat first."

Lewis nodded. He was already scanning the menu. Matt didn't need the menu, so instead he picked up the newspaper that the old man had left behind.

He jumped when a hand fell on his shoulder.

"Good grief," Daisy said mildly. "You're nervous today."

"I didn't see you come in."

"You're both all bitten up." Daisy stood next to the booth. She wore the summer uniform of the Royal Canadian Mounted Police, dark navy slacks with a yellow stripe, plus a gray, short-sleeved shirt. He felt more conscious than usual of her gun. "Where have you been?"

"We were walking on the beach trail." He could tell her now. No, Lewis had that right. "Are you here for lunch?"

"Breakfast," Daisy said. "That or lunch." She looked at her watch. "I guess it's lunchtime." She flashed him a quick smile. "I'm going to the Ladies'. If your dad comes around, ask him to pour me a cup of coffee at the counter."

Matt watched as Daisy headed off to the washroom—to comb back her short blonde hair, probably. Matt sometimes wondered whether Daisy thought she looked more official that way. If so, it was a losing battle. No matter what she did, curls always started forming near her ears. She wouldn't be through her meal before they were sneaking up her neck.

"We could tell her about the suitcase," Lewis whispered.

"Let her have her lunch first, okay? This isn't exactly an emergency." Also, they hadn't eaten yet. Once they told her about the money, chances were they'd be questioned.

As Daisy took a stool at the counter, Matt glanced back. His dad was aware that she was there, all right, even if he wasn't looking in her direction.

Abruptly Matt stiffened. "Look!" He pointed at an article on the front page. It was about the man who had died on the beach three days before. *Known Drug Trafficker in Potts*. The article gave his name, Charles Swenson. He had been almost sixty years old and he had a long criminal record.

Both boys stood. "Leave the suitcase under the table," Matt said in a low voice. "Stay nearby." He moved to Daisy's side at the counter and slipped the newspaper in front of her. "Is this the guy from the other day in the park?" he asked casually. This time he was talking to her as a Mountie, not as his dad's friend.

"Umm." Daisy didn't often discuss police matters.

"So he was a criminal?"

"He spent some time in jail during his life, yes," she said carefully. "But he died of a heart attack." She tapped the paper. "There's no reason to believe that he was doing any business here. Potts is pretty small potatoes, after all. And even criminals take vacations."

"But he could have . . ." He let the question trail off.

"What?"

"I don't know. He could've been doing drug stuff."

"Could've."

Jack came behind the counter. "Hi, lady constable. What can I do for you today?"

His father had a slow, special smile he always saved for pretty tourists who came into the café, as if they shared a secret. Lately Matt had been trying to imitate him in front of his mirror at home.

Jack was using *that* smile, gazing straight into her eyes.

Daisy just looked away. She examined the menu before setting it down. "How about coffee and a Danish?"

He frowned. "Did you eat breakfast this morning?"

"No," she said. "I did not eat breakfast. I'd like my coffee. A cinnamon bun is okay if they're fresh. Please."

"I've told you that you should always have a decent breakfast." He fired an order back to the cook, even though breakfast was technically no longer served. Eggs. Fruit. The balding cook looked out, saw who it was, and tsk-tsked. After conferring, the two men decided to allow Daisy her cinnamon bun as long as she promised to clean her plate. Jack returned to the counter. "You can still have one cup of coffee."

Daisy sighed in an exaggerated way. "Why do you bother asking me what I want?"

"Habit." He seemed to notice Matt again. "Sorry, son, you said you wanted to discuss something."

Matt and Lewis exchanged glances. "It's not important anymore," Matt said.

Lewis nodded. He didn't say anything, but as he returned to the booth, he had a wild look in his eyes like his clothes were full of bugs and he didn't dare scratch. Barely able to contain his excitement, Matt headed toward the door. Lewis followed right behind, bottles clunking.

"Matthew," Jack called when they were just inside the coat area. "Wait right there."

Matt froze. His father knew. *Matthew* was a dead giveaway.

Neither boy moved as Jack joined them in the entranceway. Neither boy breathed.

"Look, Matt," Jack said in a low voice. "You and Lewis are always welcome at the café. But I expect you to wear clean clothes. Your pants are filthy, and you left sand in the booth. Go clean it up." His eyes were kind as he turned toward Lewis. "It looks like you found quite a haul today." Lewis nodded, his eyes wide. "Next time, leave your bottles outside, all right?"

MATT CLEANED THE area in record time. "Sorry, Dad," he said as he emptied the dustpan and hurried toward the door.

"Are you coming back for lunch?" Jack called after him.

"Later!"

Both boys filled their lungs as soon as they got outside. "Half," Lewis managed. "You get half."

Matt felt sick, like when he was five and he threw up at his birthday party.

It looks like somebody ate too much cake.

The man in the park. A drug dealer. A suitcase full of money. It all fit together.

His breath was coming normally now. Matt began to grin. Things couldn't be better. Drug money didn't belong to anybody except maybe some crime lord in South America. He knew that from watching TV.

They were rich.

C H A P T E R
3

LATER MATT TRIED TO REMEMBER WHEN AND HOW they decided that they wouldn't tell any adults. Lewis didn't trust anyone in his family. As for Matt . . . a couple of years previously, he had inherited ten thousand dollars from his grandfather. That ten thousand was in a trust fund somewhere. For his education, Jack said, because that was the way his grandfather wanted it.

This money wasn't going to end up in an old bank vault. He wanted to spend it. Now.

"I'm starving," Lewis said after they had the money drying on Matt's floor. They had counted it, each of them sitting on one of the twin beds. $400,000.

"There's some pepperoni pizza in the freezer." Matt grinned. "I have an idea."

WHILE THE OVEN was heating, he held the plastic ketchup container carefully in his hands as he squeezed a thin S on the still-frozen pizza and then drew a line through it:

"How's that?" he asked Lewis.

"Ketchup on pizza?"

"The design."

Lewis looked more closely. "Matt, you put *ketchup* on pizza."

They ate too fast, because Matt kept pretending the pizza was money, so Lewis had to pretend the same. As soon as they were through, they cleared up the kitchen and headed back upstairs.

"It sure is hot in here." Matt reached down into the suitcase. He began fanning himself with money as he leaned back against the headboard. Suddenly something struck him in the cheek. "Ow!" He swung around.

Lewis was folding one of the hundreds into a small paper airplane. "This paper is perfecto." He aimed at the opposite wall. The little plane hit Matt's U2 poster and fell to the floor.

For a while they sat there making planes. One plane began to soar out the open window, and Matt nearly knocked himself out leaping after it. It fell short, dropping behind his radiator. He and Lewis stared at each other. "We have to be careful," Matt said, speaking for both of them.

Lewis nodded, wide-eyed.

After that, both lay on their respective beds. Matt covered himself with money like he was going to take a nap, and Lewis did the same. Hundred-dollar bills smoothed the bare flesh of his legs. Hundreds nudged his feet. Hundreds covered his chest. His head lay on more hundreds on the pillow (which frankly wasn't that comfortable). He felt like Scrooge McDuck.

"Lew, what are you going to buy first?" No answer. "Lew?" As he turned to face his friend, hundreds fell from his pillow onto the floor.

Lewis was staring straight up at the dots in the ceiling. Judging from his expression, he was having a really tough time deciding what to get. Either that or he was about to cry.

No, Matt decided as he settled back. That didn't make a whole lot of sense. "I'm going to buy a car," he said.

Lewis's voice was flat. "You can't drive for two years."

"Maybe a limo." He could hire a driver. He pictured Sara's expression when he drove up to Wong's Market in his limo. He'd buy his own Slurpee machine, one that worked. One with good flavors. His favorite was Orange Crush. "What about you?" he asked. "What are you going to get?"

Again, no answer.

Matt's grandmother sometimes said "a penny for

36

your thoughts." Maybe Lewis would sell his for a hundred dollars.

"I know what I want," Lewis said at last.

A mountain bike. He expected Lewis to say that he wanted a new bike.

"A computer," Lewis said softly. "An IBM, or some kind of souped-up clone."

Matt used his father's computer for games. More games would be good. He almost missed Lewis' next words.

"Spending the money could be a problem."

Matt grinned. "Speak for yourself."

"How do we explain where we got it?"

Matt sat up to straighten the hundreds on his legs, then let them fall as he grabbed another stack from the suitcase and ripped off the band. "We'll say we went out and it started to rain money."

He threw the whole stack—fifty bills—at Lewis. Hundreds flew like feathers.

"Hey!" His friend ducked. Lewis grabbed a stack.

They threw money at each other until bills were flying all over the room. Each armed himself with more money, taking shelter behind the beds. Aircraft—hastily folded hundreds—joined the seige.

Bam! Bam! Bam! Matt's bedroom door quaked.

"What's going on in there?" his father demanded from the hallway.

"Nothing," Matt called as the money began to

settle. Lewis swatted at a hundred-dollar bill that brushed his face, as though it were a pesky insect.

"For nothing, it's blasted noisy."

"We were just messing around."

His father moved away from the door. "I don't know what you two are doing inside on a nice day like this."

"Throwing money at each other," Matt said in a low voice.

Lewis flattened another hundred over his own mouth like a gag to smother his laughter. It almost worked.

His dad's footsteps retreated down the hall. Both boys sagged against Matt's bed. They looked at each other. "It's okay now," Matt said. "He won't come in."

Matt could always count on privacy in his room. He had his grandparents to thank for that. Apparently when Jack was young, his parents had insisted on checking up on everything he did. Jack had vowed that if he ever had a kid, that kid would have a space that was all his.

"Do you want to stay over tonight?" Matt asked. "If Jack says it's okay, I mean." Jack always said it was okay.

Lewis nodded. "I'll call my mom." Lewis' mom always said it was okay for him to stay with Matt. He stayed there so often that she had bought Lewis an extra toothbrush to keep at Matt's house, a pink one she found at another garage sale. She *said* she bought it in its package, never used.

It still hadn't been used.

Matt made a decision. He'd cover himself with money and fall asleep that way. He wondered what kind of dreams he'd have with hundreds all over him. He started gathering up the bills. Lewis just stood there. "What?"

"Nothing." Lewis reached down to pick up money that had fallen behind the bed. "Your dad's okay, that's all." His voice was gruff.

Matt knew his dad was okay. He thought Lewis' dad was basically okay, too, at least when he wasn't drinking. Mr. Rannulf knew all kinds of things about carpentry and fishing that he enjoyed explaining whenever Matt asked him a question. Maybe if Lewis asked him questions sometimes, they'd get along better.

Lewis begrudgingly admitted that things were better at home since Mr. Rannulf had joined AA. But that didn't mean that he had stopped being mad at his father. It probably didn't help Lewis to forget when he had to wear his broken glasses.

"I'll go call," Lewis said and headed downstairs.

Matt straightened the silver-framed picture of his mother that had fallen flat on the dresser while they were scuffling. At least it hadn't broken. The glass was dusty, so he wiped it on his shirt. The picture was always there, but he seldom really looked at it. He looked at it now.

His mother had been slender with pale hair. He couldn't remember her any more than he could remember being the two-year-old she held. Not really. Sometimes he'd hear a fragment of a soft song at the park when a mother was singing to her baby, and he'd look around. Or a woman's flowery perfume would bring tears to his eyes for no reason at all. His mother was smiling in the photograph, but there was something about her that seemed fragile, as though a light breeze might carry her away.

Maybe it had. She had died of pneumonia when he was five.

Lewis' feet pounded back upstairs. "It's okay with Mom," he said. "Your dad says I can stay, but you'll have to make dinner because he's going out."

Matt had forgotten that Jack had a date with Daisy. "Great! We can have the other pizza."

"No ketchup this time," Lewis said severely.

He'd already done ketchup. This time he'd use mustard.

Matt looked once more at the fair-haired woman in the picture before setting it back on the dresser. Daisy was blonde, too, but the comparison between the two women stopped there. Daisy was built to last. She lifted weights and jogged. She took part in police games held in the city and had had her picture in the paper a few months earlier for winning a shooting trophy.

He wondered whether his mom would have liked Daisy.

LEWIS SAID THEY should act normal while Jack was there. At that time of day, *normal* meant sitting in front of the TV. *Normal* didn't mean concentrating on commercials, but that's what they did.

A Club Med vacation was being advertised, some place with an impossibly blue ocean. "I don't think so," Lewis said.

A special at Taco Bell. "Sounds good."

A sporty red car pulled up to a hotel. "That's for me," Matt said.

Both boys lost interest when the program came on. They were waiting for the next round of commercials.

"I don't believe it," Jack said when he came in and looked over their shoulders. "You're watching an educational program."

Was he? Matt didn't even know what was on. He focused on a gigantically blown-up picture of a caterpillar.

"I almost forgot," Jack apologized too heavily. "Lewis is with you."

"Lewis is a brain," Matt chanted softly after his father left the room. *Lewis is a good influence.* Jack said it was like Lewis was an anchor and Matt was a sail. Without Matt, Lewis didn't go anywhere. Without Lewis, Matt would fly up into the stratosphere.

"Your father is okay," Lewis said again.

No ONE DRESSED up in Potts, but Jack was wearing a jacket that night, taking Daisy to dinner at a new sea-food restaurant overlooking the wharf. "I don't want you two staying up late," he said as he checked his tie in the hallway mirror.

"It's summer," Matt protested.

Jack grabbed his car keys. "Instead of watching television, why don't you play a game? Not Nintendo, a board game."

Both boys moaned softly. A bored game sounded about right.

"I heard that. You have lots of games. There's Sorry. Or Monopoly. Or Klondike."

Lewis sat straight up. "Monopoly!"

Matt was thinking the same thing.

GO TO JAIL. GO DIRECTLY TO JAIL. DO NOT PASS GO. DO NOT COLLECT $200.

"Darn," Matt said and almost killed himself laughing. "I don't collect two hundred dollars."

"You don't buy anything, either." On his next throw, Lewis landed on Pacific Avenue. He put three hundred-dollar bills into the bank. Real hundred-dollar bills. Then he tossed again. "Are you having a good time in jail?"

"It's okay. Maybe I'll get a tattoo."

"No more prison jokes, okay?" Lewis said. "It's not that funny." He landed on Mediterranean, which cost sixty dollars. All they had were hundreds. "We need change."

"Use Monopoly money." Too bad. A game played completely with real money would be truly great.

Lewis paid. "We still need change." He paused. "Which one of us is going to walk into the bank and get some?"

The real bank was closed. It was definitely closed. "Don't look at me." Matt put two hundreds into the Monopoly bank so he could get out of the slammer. This time he landed on Community Chest. "I won second prize in a beauty contest."

"That figures."

"You know what?" Matt said as he took his prize money. "I bet that if we did play with all real money, pretty soon it would feel like Monopoly money."

Lewis nodded grimly. "Until we spend it, that's exactly what it is."

THEY WATCHED MORE TV, then talked into the night. Matt was feeling really good. Lewis didn't even spoil his mood when he started talking about the guy who died. The way Lewis figured it, the man had probably either been buying drugs or selling them. He had either already met somebody or he was planning to meet him. Chances were good that somebody would miss him.

Matt yawned. Somebody might come looking for the guy who'd been carrying the suitcase, sure.

Not for two kids.

THE NIGHT WAS hot, too hot for either a blanket or a sheet. Too hot to cover their legs with money, which shifted and tickled their mosquito bites. Matt finally ended up shaking his money onto the floor, after Lewis piled his up neatly next to the bed. He had heard Jack come back awhile ago. Sometimes Daisy came in with him, but not tonight.

He started to drift off. "You could buy new glasses," he whispered after they'd been quiet for a while. "New clothes. Dad says you're bound to grow sometime."

Lewis didn't say anything.

Matt turned over on his side. "Are you mad?"

"No," Lewis said clearly. "I'm asleep."

With anybody else, this would be a joke. Not Lewis. He was breathing slow and easy.

"G'night," Lewis mumbled.

" 'Night." Jeez. Matt closed his eyes and continued the list that he'd started on the trail.

Shoes. There were some very sharp shoes in the

mall. When he had showed them to Jack, his father exploded and said that his first car hadn't cost that much. Matt ended up having to hear the whole lecture on how running shoes used to be cheap.

Maybe he and his dad could go for a vacation somewhere. It would be okay if Daisy came along. She said she enjoyed camping. Personally, Matt leaned toward Disneyland.

Disneyland and Universal Studios.

Yeah!

No!

He had started to drift off, but suddenly he came wide awake. He couldn't take Jack on a vacation if he couldn't tell him about the money. Couldn't get his dad a great birthday gift.

This whole money thing might be more complicated than he thought. Matt settled back uneasily. Lewis wasn't the only person who could think. He had a brain, too.

They needed jobs, Matt thought and almost laughed. Then he yawned so hard that his jaw cracked. He must be really tired, he decided as he pulled up the sheet. Everything had changed since that morning and he was back in rerun mode.

He fell asleep with the two words changing in his head like traffic lights.

Money.
Jobs.
Jobs.
Money.

C H A P T E R
4

THE NEXT MORNING, THEY EACH TOOK FIVE HUNDRED dollars and went on the ferry to the city of Vancouver.

They spent that entire day at Playland and rode all the rides except the kiddy ones. Both of them got their noses royally sunburned. Both ate so much ice cream and other junk that they couldn't go on the roller coaster for a fifth time. Afterward they went into an electronics store and bought Walkmans. Matt got a portable CD player, too, and a bunch of CDs. Lewis didn't see any point, since he couldn't bring anything home.

While they waited downtown for the bus back to the ferry, Lewis wandered over to the window of a shop that sold eyeglass frames. As he looked over the display, he fingered the black tape that held his glasses together at the top of his nose.

He turned and walked away without saying anything.

THEY ARRIVED AT Horseshoe Bay almost an hour early. Matt was about to suggest that they sit in the small park area outside the terminal, but Lewis was already charging toward the ticket booth. He slapped his money on the counter, glared back, and then went through the door into the long passageway.

That gave Matt two choices. He could stay where everything was green and sunny and people smiled at each other. Or he could join Lewis in the tunnel-like docking area.

"Where to?" asked the woman behind the register.

"Potts." The door buzzed. Matt went through. He took his time walking down to the foot passenger area.

As expected, he found Lewis standing outside, leaning against one of the wide pillars holding the overhead loading ramps. He was staring out to sea. Nobody else was in sight.

The last cars were just clattering up the metal ramp onto the Bowen Island ferry as Matt set down his pack.

"Want to get a cola?" A waiting area nearby had vending machines and washrooms.

Lewis shrugged.

Both boys watched the ferry pull out. Lewis' voice was soft when he finally spoke. "I say we should turn the money in. It's dirty."

Aw, man. "Because of where it came from?"

Lewis nodded.

Matt searched for the right words. "Hey, it's not like we're going to use it to buy drugs." Or weapons or whatever else it would have been used for.

"One stinking day at Playland . . . that's all we can do with it."

"We can probably afford two days." It was a joke.

Lewis didn't laugh. "I say we turn it in. Either that, or you take it."

Matt searched Lewis' face to see if he was serious. "Are you crazy? How can I spend $400,000 by myself?"

"I can't spend it *at all*. If I buy new glasses, I'll have to keep them in a drawer." Lewis didn't even blink when Matt suggested that he put his half away for college. He stood there, kicking at the pillar with the toe of one shoe and shaking his head. "I have to think about this."

"It's money," Matt cried in frustration. "It's free money."

"OH, MY."

Matt had stood beside jackhammers. He'd gone with Lewis to watch man-sized boulders being dynamited into pebbles. But never in his entire life had he heard anything as loud as those two words from the elderly woman who walked toward them from the other side of the pillar.

Both boys froze. There was no way she couldn't have heard them. It was all over. Just like that.

"Let's get out of here," Lewis said in a low voice.

"You're the boy from the café," the woman said before Matt's legs would obey him. *"I know your father."*

It wasn't his imagination—she really was speaking loudly. He cast a pleading look at Lewis. She knew him. Running away and taking a later ferry wouldn't help. "Yes, ma'am."

She frowned. He watched, spellbound, as she adjusted something near her ear. "That's better," she said in a normal voice. "I always turn off my hearing aid while the ferries are loading." She paused. "I was admiring your sunburned noses. I believe I'm carrying some ointment." She began to dig in her purse. "So, what have you two been up to? Out spending your money?"

Most of Matt's bags were in his pack, but the largest bag with the electronics store logo lay on the ground next to his feet. She was looking straight at it. "We went to Playland," Matt managed. His throat had completely dried up.

Lewis' voice shook when he finally spoke. "Matt's dad . . . his birthday is in a couple of weeks."

Matt hadn't thought of his dad's birthday that day, not once. Lewis was making it sound like the CD player in the bag was a gift.

She winked at them. "I won't say a word."

CHAPTER
5

FOUR DAYS LATER, MATT AND LEWIS WERE SQUATTING on the floor of Matt's room staring at forty stacks of hundred-dollar bills. Each stack contained ten thousand dollars. Sometimes they arranged the money in eighty stacks; sometimes they tried to see how high it would go before toppling.

"This is dumb," Matt said. "At this rate, we're right back where we started last week. *'We need jobs,'* " he mimicked. " *'We need money.'* "

Lewis was sitting very still. "We need jobs," he said.

That's where they were a week ago, all right.

"We need jobs," Lewis said again except more loudly this time. He stood up. *"We need jobs."*

Maybe the strain was getting to him. Matt held out one hand toward his friend. "Hey, it's okay."

"Jobs," Lewis repeated. He batted away Matt's hand. "If we had jobs, then we'd have an excuse for having money."

"But we don't have jobs."

"Wait." Lewis turned around in a complete circle

51

like he'd lost sight of Matt. "We only have to look like we have jobs."

"How do you look like—" Matt stopped. "You mean like, we could say we have paper routes." The only problem with that was that the local distributor came into the café.

Lewis was far ahead of him. "Not paper routes. Look, we'll ride around. I bet we can find jobs by the end of the day."

"But not real jobs." An awful thought occurred to him.

With their luck, just when they didn't want a genuine job, they'd probably find one.

THEY BIKED TO Upper Potts. "What do you think we should look for?" he asked Lewis after they passed Joneson Park.

"It's not what," Lewis said definitely. "It's who."

"Who?" They stopped at the light, one of two in town. After that point, either they went straight ahead or else up Blackberry Hill. Most of the fast-food places were up the hill. Nearer were small stores of all kinds, a butcher shop, a sporting goods place, a stationery store. "What do you mean, who?"

"It has to be somebody who might hire us. It has to be both of us. Otherwise, things get too complicated. Oh, yeah. It has to be somebody who isn't likely to deal with our parents."

That narrowed things down. Almost everybody in town dropped into the café at some time. Lewis' dad had worked for a lot of people, if only for short periods. Sometimes Lewis' mom worked as a taxi dispatcher.

The light changed, but they didn't move. "Maybe we could make up somebody," Matt said uneasily.

Lewis shook his head as cars went past them. "They'd know."

The light changed again. Slowly they walked across the street toward the road which would take them up Blackberry Hill. Matt glanced across the street, at Wong's. Sara was outside arranging bouquets of flowers in green plastic buckets.

"Hey, Sara!" Matt waved.

The girl shaded her eyes. After a moment's hesitation, she gave him a brief wave. She went back into the store.

Matt felt deflated. She didn't remember him. On the other hand, maybe the sun was in her eyes. "I'm beginning to feel thirsty," he announced.

"We're not buying another Slurpee from Wong's," Lewis said sourly. Abruptly he stared at the market. "Wong's. *Okay.*"

Wong's? Okay? "Uh, Lewis?"

The light changed. Lewis headed across the street with real speed and determination. "Just follow me."

He followed. "What are we doing?"

"Getting drinks."

"That's all? Just drinks?"

"I'm thinking."

Lewis couldn't talk and think at the same time. Pedaling seemed to give him some trouble, too. He got off and walked his bike the rest of the way, whistling under his breath.

They passed the rows of souvenir T-shirts displayed outside the market and rested their bikes against the brick wall. As they entered, Matt looked around. Wong wasn't in sight.

Lewis marched straight toward the store's cooler and took out an Orange Crush. "Good move," Matt said. Even Wong couldn't mess up something that came already in a can.

Sara came around one of the aisles. She headed behind the counter to take their money. This time there was no sun in her eyes. She really didn't recognize him.

"Hi," Matt said. "I was in here the other day."

"You both were," she said. "I remember."

She didn't sound like she thought it was very important. Matt cleared his throat. "Well, I'm Matt—"

Lewis grabbed a paperback book from the rack next to the magazines, another fantasy. The cover featured a troll in a horned helmet. "I want to buy this, too."

"Oh, that's a good one," Sara said. "I read it. Your name is Lewis, right?" She smiled at him, and that jolted Matt.

"You're Sara Lee," Lewis said.

The girl shook her head slightly and her long black hair rippled on her shoulders. "Do you like Terry Brooks?"

Lewis liked Terry Brooks. The two talked about Terry Brooks for a few minutes while Matt just stood there.

"So," she finally said, "did you two find jobs?"

"No," Matt answered.

"Is Mr. Wong here?" Lewis asked.

"He'll be right back."

"We've been thinking." Lewis started to pop the tab on his soda, then hesitated. "We want to see if we can work here."

Sara took a step backward. "Hey, my uncle's not hiring, okay? Sorry."

"We figure on working for nothing," Lewis said.

Matt stared at him. "Right," he echoed, wondering what his friend had in mind. It wasn't like they needed the money, but this was ridiculous. "We'll work for free."

"Why?" Sara asked, saving him the trouble.

"We need experience. Maybe we can't find paying jobs this year, but if we work at the market, we'll get experience stocking shelves and cleaning and things. All we ask is that if we do all right, we get decent recommendations." Lewis paused for breath.

Matt jumped in. "You're probably not used to

living in a small town. People here know the kids who get into trouble. Your uncle knows we're responsible and stuff like that. I've worked in my dad's café."

"I make good grades," Lewis said, as if that meant something. "And I can count cash really fast."

Matt almost cracked up, so he had to turn away. The only cash Lewis had ever counted was sitting on the floor of his bedroom.

Sara looked confused. "But no pay—" She stopped. "My uncle is the only one who can decide."

Since their cans of pop had almost stopped sweating, they went outside to drink and wait for Wong to return. They were just finishing when Wong drove up in his station wagon.

They didn't follow him in right away, to give Sara a chance to talk with him. Then they hung around just inside the door.

Matt wished he understood Chinese. He thought Sara was on their side even though she looked confused. Wong kept glancing toward him and gesturing as if he couldn't figure out what was happening. Matt almost felt sorry for him, because he'd obviously never been presented with two prime specimens beating down his door to work for him gratis.

Finally Sara came over to them. "My uncle says—" She stopped and turned to say something else in Chinese to Wong. A pleading note was in her voice. His answer was short. Her hair whipped back again.

"I'm supposed to tell you that I have a boyfriend in the city." She looked embarrassed.

Matt's cheeks warmed. Wong figured he wanted to work there to get close to his niece. Behind the counter, the man was watching them carefully.

He couldn't think of anything to say, not a single word.

"We figured you'd have three or four boyfriends," Lewis said easily.

Matt gulped. "At least."

Sara seemed to relax. "Just one. But steady."

That seemed to settle things for Wong. He called Sara back and talked to her for a while.

She returned to them. "Okay, this is the way it's going to be. You'll start working half days in the afternoon, never alone. You don't get near the cash and you don't eat anything without permission. If you stick it out a month and you do a good job, you get references."

"Great!" Matt cried.

Lewis hadn't moved. "One condition," he said.

Sara and Wong tensed. Matt froze.

"We don't want you to tell anybody we're working free. I don't think anybody will ask. It's just that this might sound stupid to a lot of people and we don't want to be laughed at."

Another consultation. Wong nodded.

"You're on," Sara said. "You can start tomorrow."

Matt and Lewis didn't dare look at each other until they were out and clear of the store. They got on their bikes and flew up Blackberry Hill toward the arcade.

They had jobs to go with their money.

Yes!

CHAPTER

6

ON THEIR FIRST DAY, MATT ALMOST STARTED LAUGHING when Wong refused to let them anywhere near the cash register. He didn't leave them for one minute with anything more valuable than the brown aprons he gave them to wear over their jeans and T-shirts. Like he thought they were going to walk off with his supply of jawbreakers.

Like they couldn't afford to buy their own gumball factory. Okay, other stuff was behind the counter besides the cash register. Cigarettes. Videotapes. Lottery tickets.

They could buy all of Wong's lottery tickets and all of his videotapes and his whole store.

No. In his wildest daydreams, Matt could not envision buying a Chinese market. A Chinese restaurant, maybe.

Something occurred to him as he was stocking shelves with tins of baby corn. He began to wonder how people harvested baby corn.

Whether you could eat baby corn on the cob.

Whether anybody ate baby popcorn at the movies while watching short subjects.

A laugh began to tickle his throat like dust. (There wasn't a lot of dust. The store was very clean.) No more than a snort escaped before Lewis was at his side. He crouched next to Matt like he was helping him. "How are we supposed to keep this job if you can't even keep a straight face?"

"Sorry."

Matt tried to think sad thoughts.

Through the high windows he could hear kids outside on their bikes, goofing around. They were free. He used to be free, too, but that was two weeks ago, when he was broke. He could be out with them if he didn't have so much money.

"It'll be better once we get a routine established," Lewis said, rising.

Matt sighed and stacked more tins from the box.

HE WAS ALMOST surprised to see how quickly Lewis adjusted to working there. They had only been in the store a few hours before he rearranged the hodgepodge of wicker baskets near the windows. That earned him a curt nod of approval.

He supposed Lewis couldn't help being the way he was, but this was not Matt's idea of the way to spend his summer vacation.

ON THEIR SECOND day, before they reported for work, Lewis went into the eyewear shop at the mall to try on frames. Two weeks' pay, that's how much he figured new glasses would cost. Two weeks' pay if he was being paid the amount a kid might reasonably earn.

Meaning that Matt was stuck there for a minimum of two weeks. He didn't mind the work exactly, but he wished that Sara Lee would talk to him about something other than the location of the broom and dustpan.

AT HOME, THEY decided to store the money in the bottom of the old toy trunk in Matt's bedroom. With board games on top of the money, and baseball equipment on top of that, nobody could guess what was on the bottom.

ON THE THIRD day, members of Wong's family came to look them over. Wong's old mother brought the two children, a girl around kindergarten age and a boy who looked about two years old. Lewis had found out from Sara that Wong's wife was born in Canada. She worked as a technician at the hospital.

When the baby saw his father, he raised his arms and bounced in his grandmother's arms. The girl had already beaten him into Wong's lap. She made a sly face at her brother, whose thumb went promptly into his mouth. Wong moved the girl to one knee so he had room for the second child. Matt was frankly surprised to see Wong as a doting father, since he always seemed so grim when kids came into the store.

The grandmother stood watching Matt and Lewis for a long time, then smiled in a way that made the skin crinkle around her eyes. She reached into a plastic container and handed them each a chocolate Tootsie Pop. It was weird, but for a second Matt felt like he actually *was* being paid.

After that, Wong allowed them slightly more room.

SARA'S ATTITUDE CONTINUED to rankle. She and Lewis talked easily enough, but despite Matt's best efforts to be friendly, she stayed offhand and correct with him even when Wong went out.

Especially when Wong went out.

Matt suspected her antagonism had something to do with her boyfriend in the city. Every day when things were slow, he'd see her sitting behind the counter writing long, long letters. She always used a notebook with a clip to hold her pale pink notepaper. Her handwriting was very small.

Matt happened to come around an aisle once as she was finishing a letter. She wrote LOVE in huge letters, taking almost half a page, and filled the rest with X's. Then she spotted Matt looking at her. Sara closed the notebook quickly. "What's the matter?" she snapped. "Did you run out of things to do?"

"HE LOOKS LIKE you," Lewis said later, after Sara handed Matt a broom and he went off, whistling, to sweep up near the section where they kept the briquettes.

"Who does?"

"The guy Sara keeps writing to. I saw his picture. He's older, seventeen or eighteen. But he looks something like you."

"Yeah?" Matt looked over his shoulder toward the front of the store, where Sara was sitting at the counter.

"I'm not positive," Lewis went on, "but I think her family sent her here this summer to get them apart for a while."

Ve-r-r-r-ry interesting. "How come you know all this?"

Lewis shrugged. "She talks to me."

SHE EVEN TALKED to Matt sometimes.

Matt had been sure he'd expire from boredom once he finished reading the messages on the caps hanging from the rafters. The truth was that he found the store more interesting than he could have imagined. He wasn't picking up Chinese words like Lewis, but he was finding out all sorts of great stuff.

For one thing, he had never seen so many kinds of

tea in his life. Reading the labels on some of Wong's teas was like reading the claims for old patent medicines. "Is this stuff any good?" he asked Sara the next time she came near while he was straightening the boxes on the tea shelf.

"Sure." She shrugged. "If you like tea."

He lifted out a green box of tea. "There's this old lady who comes into the café. She used to baby-sit me. She has arthritis in her hands, and I guess it's really getting bad. She's always spent a lot of time in her garden, but now she says she might have to hire somebody." He tossed the box into the air and then caught it. "So I figured this would be worth the price if it does some good."

For the first time since they started working there, Sara looked at him carefully. "I don't think it will do her any harm," she said at last. "And she'd probably appreciate the thought." She took out a slim orange box. "This doesn't cure anything, but it smells awfully nice."

"Jasmine?" He took it from her. "Maybe I should get both. My grandmother's birthday is coming up."

Lewis appeared from around the counter. "Hey, Cheesecake," he called to Sara. "Customers." He walked up to Matt as she hurried toward the front. "What were you two talking about?"

"Tea," Matt answered.

SARA CONTINUED TO write to her boyfriend every day, but Matt didn't know how often the guy wrote back. A couple of times he saw her unfolding a letter with a couple of lines on it and sighing. Even after they'd been there two weeks, it looked to him like she kept folding and unfolding the same letter.

AN AFTERNOON ARRIVED when Wong and his family went swimming.

Sara had volunteered to stay at the store and watch the counter. Although she didn't say it in so many words, Matt didn't think Wong would have left unless some family member stayed behind. Matt could hardly believe they were going, because it seemed to him that Wong never did anything but work.

It wasn't like they had never been left alone at the store with Sara during the two weeks they had been there, but this would be for the entire afternoon.

Matt felt honored. They were trusted.

The Wongs stopped by the store to pick up cases of pop before heading out to the beach. Mrs. Wong had the day off from the hospital, so she was there, wearing shorts and a straw hat with a pink ribbon. All of them wore hats of one kind or another. The little girl kept taking hers off to look at it. Wong had taken a Blue Jays' baseball cap from the rafters.

The baby was wearing a shirt that kept riding up to show his fat belly. Lewis leaned down to talk to him in his own language, Chinese baby talk. All Matt could think of to do with the baby was to press his belly. It was like putting a finger in rising bread dough except that rising bread dough didn't giggle at you.

Wong asked whether they had any questions.

Matt had one. "Do you get sunburned?"

Lewis looked at him like he was an idiot, but Matt had been wondering that for a long time about people of color.

"Yes," Wong answered, frowning.

His wife put her hand before her mouth while she translated for the grandmother. The grandmother's eyes crinkled behind pointy sunglasses that made her look like a retired Asian movie star.

"Thanks for reminding me," Mrs. Wong said as she took a container of suntan lotion from the shelves.

MATT HELPED CARRY the pop to their car, which was plenty loaded up with a huge beach umbrella. "Have a good time, boys," Mrs. Wong called as she closed her car door. "And thank you." The old grandmother waved as they left. The baby waved, too.

"Do you think we had anything to do with him taking a day off?" Lewis asked as they went back inside the store.

"Yeah." He thought so. "Yeah, I think we did."

He shook his head. A lot of things happened when you found a suitcase full of money.

C H A P T E R
7

"IT'S PAYDAY TOMORROW," LEWIS REMINDED MATT. "I'm picking up my glasses."

They had agreed to tell their parents that they were paid every other Friday. This was their second Friday, meaning that Matt could bring out something that he'd bought as long as it didn't cost very much.

"Walkman time," Matt said and yawned.

"VERY NICE," SARA said, when Lewis came in wearing his new glasses with Indiana Jones–style wire frames. Lewis had a haircut, too. Without hair to push back from his eyes, and with no tape covering the bridge of his nose, he didn't look very Lewis-like at all.

"Why, Lewis," Matt said in a falsetto voice. "You're—you're beautiful."

Lewis scowled.

"He's just jealous," Sara said.

LATER, WHEN THEY were alone, Lewis told him that his dad had offered to pay half the cost of the glasses. "He said that he didn't owe it to me, because I had a smart

67

mouth, but maybe he should have been more careful."

"Are you taking it?"

Lewis nodded. "It's the closest he'll ever come to an apology. Anyway, in another two weeks I can probably afford a good used bike. I mean, it will look like I can afford one. You know what I mean."

Another two weeks.

Unbelievably, Matt didn't really mind.

THEY USUALLY ATE during their break, carrying their bag lunches over to the shade in front of the art gallery. Lewis kept looking from side to side as if he were hoping that someone would come over and tell him how great he looked.

They were just finishing as Dermot the Hermit came up and began tacking another poem on the community bulletin board. He stood back, stroking his beard, then turned away.

"I liked the one about the seagull," Lewis called.

He didn't hear.

"He probably doesn't think that anybody reads his poems," Matt said.

"Lots of people do." Lewis stood and went after him.

After a moment, Matt followed. "Hey, Dermot." He caught up with him and touched his sleeve.

The old man stopped and turned around with such

a fierce expression that Matt was positive he was about to have his lights punched out.

"What do you two want?" Dermot snarled.

This was one tough old man. "It's me," Matt stammered. "Matt Snow. My dad owns the Come Back Café. You eat there sometimes."

He didn't relax one bit. "So?"

"So I was just saying hi."

Dermot's lips drew back. His smile sent a chill down Matt's spine, and not just because it wasn't really a smile. Dermot had a bad scar down one side of his face. He had teeth only in front, giving him the appearance of an animal that could snap you in half with one bite.

"I saw your poem on the bulletin board," Lewis said. "I liked it."

Matt had never seen anyone change so fast. It was like when you paid a compliment to a girl, and at first she acted like you couldn't possibly be talking to her, and then she told you that you were wrong, and then she looked around like she wished she could disappear into the pavement.

"Aw, hey," Dermot said, shuffling his feet. "You don't mean one of mine."

"The one about the seagull," Lewis said. "Where he's deciding on his lunch."

The old man scratched his head. "That one wasn't

too bad." He squinted toward the sky. "We haven't had any real winds lately to knock it off the board. Maybe it disappeared into somebody's pocket."

"I guess we startled you, huh?" Matt asked.

But Dermot wasn't paying any attention to him. "What specifically did you like about that poem?" he asked Lewis.

Fortunately, he'd asked the right person. Matt would probably just answer that it made him laugh.

Lewis took a deep breath. "Well, you're talking about stuff at the dump like it's on a menu at a fancy restaurant and the seagull can't make up his mind what to choose. And to everybody reading the poem, it's all garbage."

"Bingo." The old man nodded. "You got it."

Matt and Lewis exchanged puzzled glances, but Dermot didn't seem to notice.

"Well, hell." Dermot's tone was almost friendly. "It's not meant to be any damned Shakespearean sonnet."

He must have been at the post office picking up his mail, because he showed them a booklet in a ripped manila envelope. The cover said it contained information from a publisher looking for books. "Do you two boys know about this kind of thing?"

Matt just shook his head. After a moment, so did Lewis.

"These people print books. Only they're not like

real publishers. You pay them. Some people do okay that way." His voice lowered conspiratorially. "It's costly, but I'm figuring on saving up . . . from my pension, don't you know?"

"You want to print a book of your poems?" Lewis asked.

"Isn't that a whole lot of poems?" Matt couldn't imagine reading that many poems, much less writing them.

Dermot struck his thin chest dramatically. "There's a lot of poetry in me. More than enough."

Matt looked at his watch. "We have to go back now."

He nudged Lewis, who was getting that thoughtful look again. "Come on. We don't want to get fired."

Somewhere in the distance he could hear shouts of laughter at the beach.

"Mo-mo-mo . . ."

"Say Mommy," Corinne said. "Watch my lips. *Mommy*."

Lewis lay on the bed in his room, trying to read the latest Terry Brooks fantasy, which he'd gotten from the Potts library after being on the waiting list for a long, long time.

Lots of luck. Baby Joey was standing in his crib, shaking the bars and grinning his drooling grin. "Mo-mo-mo . . ."

"Say Mommy." She drew it out. "Mo-o-o-m-m-m-my."

Lewis' mother came in, too—all four of them crowded into his postage stamp-sized bedroom. "He'll talk when he gets ready," she chided her adult daughter. "You started early and you never shut up. But that one—" She nodded toward Lewis. "He started so late that we were beginning to wonder. It turned out that he was thinking about what to say. He started off with whole sentences."

"Hey, genius," Corinne called.

Lewis looked up. "What?"

"See," Corinne said, "he answers to his name."

"Mo-mo-mo . . ." Joey was going at it again. He clutched his bars, his diapered rear end bobbing up and down like a piston engine. "Mo-mo-mo . . ."

"Mommy," Corinne said.

"*Mommy,*" Lewis' mother said. "Come on, sweetie. Say it already." She paused. "I'll tell you what. Say Nana. Come on. Nana."

"Mom," Corinne protested, "you're confusing him."

More drool. Joey showed one sparkling tooth, bounced some more.

"Mommy," Corinne pleaded.

Lewis' mom made a funny face and the baby started laughing. "*Nana,*" she said, like she'd earned it.

To heck with it. Lewis sat up. "Uncle Lewis," he said.

Joey stuck his thumb in his mouth, looking from one to the other. "Everybody's getting him all confused," Corinne wailed.

The thumb came out again, shiny. "Mo-mo-mo . . ."

"Mommy."

"Nana."

"Uncle—" Lewis stopped because he was getting evil glares in stereo.

"Mo-mo-mo . . ." They all watched the baby struggle with his first word. It was like a football game.

"Come on, sweetheart," Corinne urged. "Mommy."

"Mommy," Lewis' mom conceded. "Nana can come later."

"Mo-mo-mo . . ."

"Maybe he's saying Mama," Lewis' mom said.

"That's old-fashioned." Corinne held out her arms. "Mommy."

Lewis could see Joey forming the word. He wished the kid would get it over with so they'd let him have some peace and quiet.

"Mo-mo-mo . . ."

The word burst out of the baby.

"Money!"

Lewis rolled over and laughed and laughed.

CHAPTER
8

MATT WAS MAKING CHANGE. "ENJOY YOUR ICE CREAM."

The day was hot, so they were having a run on cones at the side window. He and Lewis were allowed to get cones for themselves when things weren't busy, but right now Matt felt like he never wanted to touch the stuff again.

He was just about to turn away from the window when he spotted Daisy walking down the street. She waved at him and came in. Matt joined her at the counter as soon as he rinsed off the scoop in the sink behind the flowered curtain.

She smiled as she took in his apron, streaked with all different flavors. "It looks like they're keeping you busy."

"Sort of. Did you catch any criminals today?"

"Naw, it's too hot for crime. Everybody's at the beach."

"How about an ice cream?" he suggested.

"Great suggestion."

She browsed through the magazines while Matt got

her a scoop of rum raisin. Sara came up to him. "I'll bet she doesn't pay," she whispered.

"No bet."

Daisy was already digging in her pocket for money. She tapped the cover of a magazine. "A guy I stopped last night said I look like Princess Di. What do you think?"

"A little," Sara said with her head cocked to one side. "I can see it."

"Did you book him anyway?" Matt asked as he handed over the cone.

She laughed. "Roadside suspension."

After receiving her change, Daisy dropped the coins into a jar on the counter. This was for a local family whose child had to be sent away for a specialized operation. Matt thought Sara looked impressed. He felt like pointing to an article in the *Potts Gazette* about those same people receiving a thousand dollars anonymously in the mail. He and Lewis had sent the money because they both knew the boy's family. That was the only cash they'd given away. So far.

Daisy waved as she went out.

"She seems nice," Sara said as she began straightening videotapes. "She's going with your dad, right?"

Right. "Too bad we weren't betting money about whether she was going to pay," Matt said.

She shook her head. "I don't bet money. Haven't

you heard about Chinese people and gambling? We start betting money, we go crazy."

He didn't think she was serious, but he wasn't sure. "We could bet something else."

"Like what?" She looked at him suspiciously.

"Kisses." He felt stupid as soon as he said it.

"Huh."

He looked away. "Well, it was a thought."

"I bet you and Lewis don't bet kisses." Her tone was teasing. "You know what else? I bet you've never kissed a girl before."

She'd lose. "How much do you want to bet on that?"

Sara was the one who backed off. In fact, she knocked against the shelf. Two cartons of cigarettes fell over.

"Oh, right," Matt said as he leaned over to pick them up. "I forgot. You have a boyfriend."

A boyfriend who didn't write.

FOR THE LAST couple of days Lewis had been really silent. Even Wong had noticed.

"I've been thinking," Lewis said when they took their break. Like he ever stopped.

As usual, they were sitting under the tree by the art gallery. "What about?" Matt asked.

Lewis reached around to scratch between his shoulder blades. He took so long to answer that Matt knew something was up. "Wong's is penny ante. I have an idea." Lewis' eyes were lighting up. "No kidding, you'll like this."

If Matt was going to like this, he shouldn't have any difficulty swallowing the last bite of his sandwich. But right now his food was staying where it was. He sort of nodded.

"Get ready for some big spending."

It took a couple of swigs of pop to get everything settled. Matt tried to look unconcerned. "How big?"

"I'm deciding what kind of computer to get."

Lewis was serious. Matt didn't see how he could be, but he was. "We can't."

"We *can*. This is good. I should have thought of this before. We were too busy trying to make it look like we had jobs so we could spend a couple hundred dollars. We should have been thinking about spending thousands."

An elderly couple was walking up the sidewalk toward the art gallery. Matt lowered his voice. "We can't spend big money. We're kids."

"That's my point." Lewis laughed to himself. "Don't you get it?"

"Get what?" Matt felt ready to choke him.

"It's simple. It's super simple." He paused. "We hire an adult."

CHAPTER
9

"LET'S TRY THIS AGAIN," THE OLD MAN SAID. "YOU SAY that you *found* a suitcase filled with money."

"Not exactly filled," Matt corrected.

Lewis cut in. "We found $200,000 in an old suitcase."

Matt crossed his fingers behind his back. He and Lewis had agreed they wouldn't give the true amount. Even so, he wondered if they weren't making a big, big mistake telling an adult.

Dermot lived north of town in a shack near the ocean. He hadn't looked particularly happy to see them before they told him why they were there.

He didn't look any more welcoming afterward. He just sat there on a big flat rock overlooking the ocean, not looking at them. "You found money."

"Right." Matt was getting impatient. "We were biking, and Lewis ran over it, and I opened it, and there it was."

"You *found* it."

He seemed hung up on that word. Suddenly Matt got it.

When Matt was eight, he had stolen a couple of action figures from a store. There was no reason to take them except that he'd spent his birthday money on something that broke right away and he believed the store owed him. When he got home, that's what he told Jack. He found the things. He remembered Jack's expression of disbelief, which was followed by a swift meeting with the store owner and equally swift justice.

Dermot was looking at him the same way now.

"We didn't steal it."

"Uh-huh." He knocked his pipe on the rock. "Well, I've never heard of any bank robberies in these parts. So I imagine you found it growing somewhere. A money tree." He looked at Lewis more closely. "You're George Rannulf's boy, aren't you?"

Lewis' eyes narrowed. "That's right."

"You look something like him. I haven't seen him around lately at any of the usual watering holes."

"He joined AA."

"Is that right?"

"Three months now."

Dermot shuddered. "Alcoholics Anonymous. I never tried that route myself. Not that I have a problem that way."

Matt had already noticed the pile of empty bottles near the outhouse. "Are you friends with Lewis' dad?" That would make a big, big difference.

"Casual acquaintances." He paused. "Your father has a sense of humor, too. Did he bite when you tried this one on him?"

"It's not a joke." Lewis was practically grinding his teeth. "And there's no way I'm ever telling—"

Dermot wasn't listening. His eyes twinkled. "There's one born every minute, boys. But I'm not it. So go play your tricks on somebody else. In fact, I might be able to recommend a couple of people who would get a big chuckle out of it."

Matt looked at Lewis and Lewis looked at him. The two boys moved away from the rock, their footsteps crunching in the rocks along the shore. "Maybe we should tell him about the dead guy," Matt said in a low voice.

Lewis shook his head.

For an old man, he had really good hearing. "What dead guy?" Dermot asked.

They both turned. Matt shielded his eyes against the brightness of the day. "The dead drug guy."

"Last month," Lewis added. "It was in the newspaper."

Dermot frowned. "I read about it. You're saying that you knew him?" His tone was almost casual. "I heard about kids involved in these things, but I thought that was in the city."

"He was *dead*," Matt said. "We never heard of him until he was dead." He gestured at Lewis. "Come on, let's go."

"Right." They had left their bikes at the top of the final steep path down to Dermot's shack.

"Wait, now, boys," Dermot called. They turned. He was striking a match on the side of the rock and lighting his pipe. "I don't believe one word you're saying, but I wouldn't mind hearing the rest of it."

They conferred for a minute, Dermot watching them from his rock and puffing on his pipe faster and faster. They both returned to stand at the base of the rock. "We figure it was his. The drug guy."

"Not his," Matt put in quickly. "Drug money."

At last Dermot nodded. "And you want to make me a proposition."

Matt tried to keep his voice casual. "We want you to spend money for us."

A halo of smoke formed over his head. "Damned kind of you."

"We want you to buy things for us that we can't get for ourselves. I want a computer."

"A car." Matt gulped. "First we need a car."

"A car?" Dermot frowned. "Unless I'm missing something, you boys aren't old enough to drive."

"We need a driver, too. Somebody to drive us places and pick stuff up."

"Right now we can't buy anything we can't carry on our bikes," Lewis explained.

"Jobs," Matt said. "We need to look like we have jobs."

Dermot held up both hands. "Slow down. First, what's in this for me?"

They'd already decided that Lewis should do the negotiating. "You said you wanted to get your poems printed in a book. We'll pay you enough so you can do that."

Appreciation grew in the old man's eyes, quickly replaced by cunning. "And how much more?"

"How much do you want?" Matt asked. Lewis kicked him and he clasped his ankle. "Jeez!"

"We talked it over," Lewis said. "Our top offer is ten thousand. Cash."

Dermot nodded. "Cash." He puffed on his pipe for a minute. "Of course, if anything happens, you have an adult and you have two kids. Guess who gets blamed."

"There's nothing to get blamed for," Matt said.

"We'd tell the police what happened."

It was weird to hear Lewis talking about the police like they were a faceless blob. Potts' police force consisted of seven uniformed officers plus two people who worked at the station.

One police officer dated his dad.

Puff, puff. "How much do baby-sitters make these days? That's so I'll know how much to charge for the time you're here."

Matt was getting angry. "How much do we charge you to use our car?" He waited. "We figured that you wanted to get your poetry printed. We thought we were doing you a favor."

That was pushing it, but he was mad.

"Come on," Lewis said. "Let's get out of here. We'll go talk to that other guy, the one I suggested first."

There was no other guy.

"Sure. At least he doesn't write poems."

They turned and began walking away slowly. Matt tripped over a rock and swore.

He turned when he heard footsteps behind them.

For an old man, he was agile, too. He'd gotten down from the rock without them hearing him.

"So," Dermot said, "how do you propose to explain my having cash to do all these wonderful things?"

Matt and Lewis grinned at each other. Yes!

They were both straight-faced when they turned back.

"You're going to win a lottery," Lewis answered.

THEY SETTLED THE details before they left. They agreed to pay for expenses—in particular, the car. Dermot wanted reimbursement for any repairs and gas. Lewis surprised Matt by saying they'd require receipts. Probably that was something he'd picked up working for Wong. Dermot just nodded.

"I have a vehicle in mind," Dermot said. "Not much for looks, but the engine should be sound. It belongs to a young man down the road. He's off to college. A panel van."

That was good. They could carry a lot in a van, and nobody would know what was inside.

"How's the mileage?" Lewis asked.

"How in hell should I know?" Dermot snapped. "Probably bad. Why? Are you planning on taking a trip?" He didn't wait for their reply. "The van should go cheap." He started moving toward the trail. "It's not far from here. The owner left it sitting in their drive with a FOR SALE sign on it." He glanced at Lewis. "I don't suppose you brought any cash with you."

"Two thousand."

"That should be enough. Give it to me."

After a moment's hesitation, Lewis handed over their money.

He didn't say anything else until they were walking their bikes toward the dirt road that led to Dermot's house. "Tomorrow we quit our jobs."

Matt had started to like working at the store. "Do we have to?"

"Do we have to?" Lewis asked like it was a joke. *"Do we have to?"*

Matt guessed they had to.

LEWIS APPROACHED WONG the next afternoon. Matt busied himself straightening shelves nearby. He caught the occasional word.

"It's outside work, mostly," Lewis was saying. "The pay is pretty good."

Wong said it would be all right if they finished off that day. "You boys are hard workers," he told both of them. "I will give you good references."

Sara Lee was a lot cooler when Matt told her. "I'm surprised you stayed this long." And then she walked away.

"I DON'T FEEL too great about this," Matt admitted as they got ready to hand in their aprons.

"Why?" Lewis looked surprised. "It's not like he was paying us. We offered to stay the rest of this week." He fell silent. "Okay, it wasn't too bad."

It was good.

Sara Lee didn't even look up as they left. She just kept writing to her boyfriend.

They got outside and there was plenty of daylight left. "At least now we'll be able to spend some of that money," Lewis said.

Matt didn't say anything. He just grabbed up his bike and took off toward home. He didn't wait for Lewis even though he yelled, didn't care if his best friend saw how fast he could go when he wasn't holding back, didn't give a damn if he left him behind in the dust.

Maybe he hit a speed record.

Probably he did. He was riding on the shoulder of the road, passing cars going down the hill. When he got to the bottom of the dip, he started passing cars coming up. He was on automatic, not really knowing where he was until he skidded down his own driveway. His hands were shaking as he got out his key and opened the side door.

Matt ran up to his room.

He took out the money.

He covered his lap with money.

He knocked it onto the floor, threw a stack at the wall, and watched hundred-dollar bills flutter like confused butterflies.

Then he sat on the bed and wrote his name in his old school notebook. A hundred times, the way he'd been doing it for the last couple of weeks. Matt $now. He wrote the dollar sign bigger.

86

His jaw set. It was a lot of fun being rich.

Money meant he could do whatever he wanted, right?

Then why did he feel so rotten?

CHAPTER
10

THE NEXT MORNING, EARLY, MATT MET HIS CAR FOR THE first time. It was parked off the dirt road above Dermot's place.

The van was fifteen years old, a dark frog green with a little tinted window on each side in back shaped like a teardrop. Inside, scuffed paneling showed that it had been used for camping, although probably not recently. It even came with a camp stove and a tiny icebox. It cost twelve hundred dollars, plus the cost of insurance and paperwork.

Matt liked it. A lot.

While they were admiring the car, Matt noticed Dermot looking them over. "You both appear fairly strong," he said. "I guess I have to figure out jobs for you to do around my place, the sort of things I'd want done if I really came into money."

"Like what?" Matt asked. He and Lewis exchanged uneasy glances.

"Clean-up, that kind of thing. Some prickle bushes taken out and burned."

That was okay.

"A little fencing around my garden patch. Painting."

"We can do that," Lewis said.

"There's another small chore I have in mind." Dermot hesitated. He turned away like he was trying to avoid looking into the sun, but not before Matt caught a wicked smile. "Ever move an outhouse?"

No amount of money was worth that, and Matt told him so.

Lewis didn't exactly volunteer, either. "Forget it."

"Well—" The poet shrugged. "No harm in trying." He looked at his watch. "Anyway, if you want us to make the next ferry to Vancouver, you'd better hop in."

The engine caught the first time. Matt exchanged glances with Lewis and gave him a thumbs-up. Lewis was right.

They had been wasting their time at Wong's.

MATT HAD NEVER been in Vancouver before when he had so much money to spend. Correction. He had, a few weeks earlier, before he had been able to take advantage of his purchasing power. Now he could buy anything he wanted. Anything.

Matt looked up at the glass towers before him. The big department stores were waiting for him to make his selection. Calling to him.

The shoppers perspiring on the streets didn't realize

that, for Matt and Lewis, it was actually Christmas.

"Computers," Lewis said. "We're here to look at computers."

Computers, sure.

Among other things.

Dermot had parked the Green Machine in a multi-level garage. "Let's just walk around a little," he advised. "Don't feel you have to buy the first piece of equipment you see."

"How about clothes?" Matt suggested as they passed windows displaying clothes for fall. He'd been growing so much that, come winter, his wrists would be extending from his sweaters. Lewis would be wearing the same parka that his mom had picked up at a garage sale two years before.

Matt looked at the lemon-yellow shirt on a mannequin. *This I can buy.*

"I want to look at computers," Lewis said.

The computer stores were straight ahead, past two blocks of major department stores and specialty shops. Past stores that sold stereo equipment. "Slow down," Matt said as they hit a window filled with boom boxes. He wasn't drooling, but it was a close thing.

He spotted a gigantic blaster he really liked, with detachable speakers. *This I can buy.*

"I'm going to suggest that you two boys split up for an hour or so," Dermot said mildly.

"Huh?" The next window featured a display of

camcorders. He'd never thought before about having his own camcorder.

A CD player with multidisc carousel. He'd thought about that, all right.

"Hey, what do you think—" Matt looked around. Lewis was slowly walking away toward the computer stores.

Dermot stood there, puffing on his pipe. "We're going to meet back here in an hour."

The heck they were. "Hey, Lew!" Matt called. "Wait up!"

Jeez! They were going to leave him behind.

His friend turned, and he hurried to catch up. Dermot strolled along behind, catching up with them at the light.

Across the street, a young woman in a short blue skirt and a red tube top leaned on the wall next to a leather goods shop, watching men go by. Smiling at any who glanced in her direction. Shifting her weight from one red high-heeled shoe to the other in a bouncy way, as if she was waiting for someone to take her dancing. As the light began to turn, a man spoke to her for a few seconds, then shook his head and moved on. She made a quick face behind his back, popped her gum, and then went back to watching traffic.

As Matt and Lewis passed, she glanced at Matt. Glanced away again. She was younger than she looked at first. High-school age.

The thought ran through Matt's mind. *This I can buy.*

"I'll be back," he told Lewis.

He was aware that his friend was watching him, open-mouthed. "Hey," Lewis protested.

Dermot put a hand on Lewis' shoulder and pointed toward a knapsack in the window of the leather goods store, trying to steer him in that direction. Lewis shrugged the hand off.

"I just want to ask her something," Matt said. Potts didn't have any prostitutes, or at least none that he knew of.

He didn't wait to see whether Lewis was still glaring at him. As he neared the girl, he was startled by the brightness of her smile. "Well, hi there," she said.

From her expression, the girl seemed really happy to see him. For a second he wondered if she might know him. Like maybe she used to live in Potts and they rode the same school bus.

She didn't. They hadn't. He'd never seen her in his life.

She seemed to be waiting for him to say something in return. "Hi." Something else. He wondered if there was a code word.

"Are you looking for company?" she asked in a low voice that he guessed was supposed to be sexy.

He felt like the time when he was six and his father took him to a petting zoo. He had been curious and looking forward to the trip, but once he was there, he felt unexpectedly fearful of touching the penned animals.

She tried again. "Are you looking for a party?"

His mind immediately went to ice cream and cake. "No, a computer store."

Her eyes looked like everybody else's except that she put more black gunk around them than the girls he knew. "A computer store?" she echoed blankly.

Her arms and legs were thin. Freckled. Now that he was directly in front of her, he could see that her front was pushed up to make it seem bigger than it was. "ComputerWorld," he blurted, taking a step back. "Is it around here?"

"Do I look like the tourist information center?" She looked both ways, then gestured with a flash of bright red fingernails. "Okay, it's up two blocks and then over to your left."

"Thank you."

She started to smile at a workman in a hard hat, so Matt walked away quickly to join the others. "She says ComputerWorld is that way."

Lewis looked cheesed. "That was a hooker!"

Matt made his eyes go wide. "You're kidding."

"That was a real hooker."

Dermot nodded. "Very likely." He didn't look fooled one bit by Matt's expression of innocence. He also didn't look like he planned to laugh at him. "There are easier ways to earn a living than working the streets, or so I've heard. Safer ways, too."

Matt glanced back as they set off again. The girl was talking to the workman as though he was the answer to her dreams. *This he did not want to buy.*

Some of the brightness had faded from the day, but his mood didn't stay down for long. Fortunately, there were a whole lot of other things that he did want to buy.

Things with a simple price tag. "Hey," he said to Lewis, "does ComputerWorld carry any games?"

LATER THAT AFTERNOON, Matt sighed with joy as he lay on the deck of the ferry, regarding the world through his new designer sunglasses. Dermot was inside getting a cup of coffee. "This is good," Matt said to Lewis. He waved his arms. "This—everything."

Although most people rode inside, on sunny days the deck was often crowded for the fifty-minute crossing. Several people recognized Matt, and a few kids from school knew Lewis. That was okay. They were with Dermot. They worked for him.

No secret.

In the back of the Green Machine were two computers, identical. Both had modems, which Lewis said they should get so they could talk to each other. Matt wasn't sure what Lewis meant about that, since they'd never needed any machines before except telephones. They always just talked. One of the computers was going to have to stay boxed since both were ending up in Matt's room. Which, he was starting to figure, was going to fill up fast.

Matt bought a VCR as well, a Japanese-made one that Dermot said looked like it had all its bells and whistles. He also bought a small color TV for his room. Lewis wanted a VCR, too, but there was no way of getting around the fact that he shared his room with a baby.

"Any chance that your sister will get back together with her husband after he gets out?" Matt asked.

Lewis was lying there with his eyes closed. "Joe calls sometimes. She hangs up on him."

"Great."

"Sometimes she cries after she hangs up on him."

That sounded more promising.

They had bought some other gadgets, too, but about the only thing Lewis could bring home was a walkie-talkie. His parents would assume it belonged to Matt.

THEY HAD CAUGHT the three-thirty ferry from Horseshoe Bay, so it was four-thirty by the time they drove up to Matt's house. Lewis wanted to try out his computer, but Jack might come home any time, so they didn't dare bring anything inside. Dermot agreed to come early the next morning and they'd carry everything up to Matt's room.

As Matt shut the front door, he felt as though someone was in the house. Like Jack was already home.

Something smelled, too, like one of their neighbors was burning garden rubbish. Or maybe old tires.

He walked quietly, not wanting to wake his father if he was taking a nap. Jack had been muttering a lot lately about being an old man, something to do with his fortieth birthday the next day.

He was startled to hear Daisy's voice. "Jack? Is that you?" She was upstairs. "You're supposed to stay away for another two hours."

Daisy was at the house, but Jack wasn't supposed to be there? Quickly Matt stowed the incriminating sunglasses in his pack. "It's me," he called back. "Matt."

He didn't like her being upstairs alone, not at all. The money was up there. Cops were trained to see things, to be observant.

"Oh, thank heavens." Her relief sounded heartfelt. "Matt, could you come up here and give me a hand?"

He barely registered the uneven sprinklings of white powder on the carpeting as he took the stairs two at a time. What he saw when he reached the top made his heart seize up.

Daisy stood beside his bedroom door, dressed in jeans and a blue T-shirt. Her hand was on the knob.

He had taken out money that morning for the trip. He couldn't remember whether he had put it away.

C H A P T E R
11

Something was different about Daisy's appearance, but Matt was too shocked at first to notice.

"That's my room." His voice squeaked for the first time in a year. He was positive that he'd left the money spread out on his bed.

She took her hand away. "I didn't go in."

Whew.

One of her hands was dusted with white powder, which extended to her elbow. Matt took in the flour sprinkled through her hair. Brown, oozy goop was splashed on her shirt, with a brown blob hanging from one hoop earring. He had already noticed a white hand-print on the seat of her jeans, as if she had slapped herself. Her T-shirt had a soup-can logo that was so thoroughly smeared, he couldn't read the brand name. "What happened?"

"I was looking for the linen closet. Downstairs—" She gestured like downstairs was across the ocean. She swallowed like she was swallowing the ocean. "In the kitchen, I made a mess. I need something to throw on it."

He had come into the house through the living room, not the kitchen. "Dad's not here?" He already knew that, but he couldn't think.

She shook her head. "I told him to stay away for a few hours. I'm making his birthday cake." She gave a laugh that sounded like she was about to cry. "I've rented rooms for years, so I don't have pans or a mixer or anything like that. I figured, well, a cake." She stared upward, blinking rapidly. "Something went wrong. Most of it is still on the counter and, oh, the walls. But it's coming down fast."

Matt was speechless.

She looked directly at him again. Her voice took on authority. "Where do you keep your old towels?"

"I'll get some for you," Matt said. He opened the door next to the bathroom. "This is the linen closet. You were one door off." Close, but no four hundred thousand dollars.

He grabbed a couple of towels and turned. Daisy took them. "I think I'll need more," she said, sounding calmer.

He took out a beach towel as the smoke detector went off. Matt tensed. If she was burning down the house, he'd have to rescue the money.

"I'll take care of it." She started toward the stairs. "If you have a couple of those, bring them down with you."

Beach towels were huge.

He brought down five.

"Wow!" Matt breathed before he could stop himself.

Something had gone really wrong. Slippery brown goo hung from the under-counter light fixture and drooled down the fridge. Daisy had preheated the oven, so more blobs were bubbling and drying on the outside of the stove. One upper cabinet was open. Inside, the dishes looked like they'd been hit by a mud slide. Rivulets slid down the cabinet doors, collecting in puddles on the counter. Some of those pools were already sinking into the carpeting in mucus-like dribbles of chocolate cake batter.

Matt tried to assess the damage. His dad's industrial-strength mixer was unplugged and covered with goop. Its beaters rested in a large stainless steel bowl which was now almost empty, although Matt was willing to bet it hadn't started out that way. Daisy had thrown a tea towel over the toaster, probably protecting it instead of her face. That was all she had managed to save. Brown-slathered apples huddled together in a wooden bowl on the counter.

Wow.

Once, when he was six, Matt had decided to make fudge. He figured it would be easy since he'd "helped" his grandmother during a visit. Jack said he would have killed him when he saw the carnage except that Matt had been in big danger of killing himself. Instead, his dad settled for feeling relieved.

Another time he made hot chocolate in the micro-wave, which was allowed. "But no marshmallows," Jack had cautioned. He and Lewis couldn't figure out why.

They found out. Marshmallows expand.

Matt thought *that* had been a mess.

Daisy had him beat six ways to Sunday.

She was already on the floor pushing towels into the space under the kitchen cupboard. She glanced up at him, her cheeks flaming. "I did warn you."

"Hey, it's not so bad." He waited for God to strike him with lightning for lying. Then he decided that God was probably up in heaven waiting to see what Matt Snow was going to do next. He decided to modify that particular lie while he turned off the oven. "I mean, it's not as bad as it looks."

He never understood what that meant, but it sounded safe.

"It could be worse," he amended.

"I know," she said as she rose and headed toward the sink to wet a towel. "Once I was in a house where a bomb went off."

"Anybody home?" Matt asked as he started wiping brown goo off the fridge.

"Not anymore," she answered after a moment.

He figured Daisy had lots of neat stories, if only he

could get her to tell them. He wondered who was responsible for cleaning up the blood and guts after a bombing. Not him.

He supposed this mess wasn't his responsibility, either.

"I guess you aren't used to our mixer," Matt said cautiously as he began unreeling paper towels from the dispenser. One of the puddles from the counter was about to blob onto the floor. He bagged it.

"I guess I'm not."

"Maybe there was too much liquid in your recipe. This mixer is really heavy-duty."

"You don't have to tell me that. Your mixer could handle concrete. It was probably offended by a simple cake." Daisy swiped at her front with the towel, smearing it more. "Everything started to spurt all over, and I couldn't see the control to turn it off. If I'd had my gun out, I would have shot it."

"Really?" Wow.

"No, not really."

She had one of Jack's simpler cookbooks open in a plastic stand, so it had stayed clean. After wiping off the stand, Matt decided from the ingredients which chocolate cake recipe she was attempting. A Black Midnight cake. That was a good one when it came out, not too sweet like other chocolate cakes. While he was thinking about it, his mouth started to get set for a piece of Black Midnight cake with vanilla ice cream.

The kitchen was really getting hot and the vent above the stove couldn't churn out the smoke fast enough. Matt opened the windows that weren't already open. Both he and Daisy leaned out for a moment to take deep breaths.

Fortunately, the refrigerator was on wheels, so he could pull it out easily. The rest of the place cleaned off easily enough, although after a while he had to go upstairs to fetch more towels.

He'd emptied the dishwasher that morning. By the time Daisy was finished clearing out the cupboard, it was full.

"Maybe I can give you a hand when you start on the cake again," Matt offered as he rinsed off the apples.

Daisy gave him a stricken look that had him wondering whether he had hurt her feelings. "Matt," she said slowly, "I really want this cake to come out well. It means a lot to me."

"Hey, I like chocolate cake, too," he protested, wondering if she thought he had never made a cake before. He stopped.

From her expression, it was obvious. She thought he had never made a cake before and that he'd mess things up. As though Jack didn't have him sifting ingredients as soon as he was big enough to stand on a chair.

A slow smile spread across his face before he could fight it back, but she was studying the recipe so she didn't notice. In his room Matt had ribbons from the Fall Fair for the past two years. The red ribbon from when he was twelve was for his carrot cake in the junior category. The blue was from last year, for baking cinnamon rolls. For that one, he competed against adults.

"Have you made a lot of cakes before?" he asked politely when she looked up.

"Sure," Daisy answered too quickly. She was standing before the newly cleaned mixer as though she was considering hand-to-beater combat. "Okay, I've made cakes from mixes. I know it's been a while, but I figured on making this one from scratch."

Matt leaned against the fridge. "My grandmother used to let me supervise." That was when he was two and they were afraid he'd stick his fingers in a socket. *Supervise* was a nice way of saying that he could look but not touch. "Would that be okay?"

After a moment, Daisy nodded. "Perhaps you could measure some ingredients. And you could tell me where things are located. I'd really appreciate that. I'm already running late."

HE'D NEVER SWEATED making a cake so much. He measured the liquids for her since that was where he figured she went wrong. He caught her looking suspiciously at him when he cracked the eggs using one hand, the way Jack did. Crack, splat, toss shells to one side, crack, splat. "Sometimes I make scrambled eggs in the morning," he said like that explained everything. "Jack showed me how to break the eggs this way. He says it impresses women every time."

"Uh-huh."

So maybe that wasn't the best thing to say.

This time, Daisy and the mixer made peace with no trouble. He watched to make sure that she was greasing the pans but not overgreasing them so Jack didn't end up with fried birthday cake. When Daisy slid the two cake pans in and closed the oven door, she shut her eyes like she was praying. "Well," she said brightly, "that's that. Maybe we should run the dishwasher."

Matt shook his head. "Vibrations," he said. She stared at him. "The dishwasher makes the floor vibrate. The cake won't rise."

"I guess you can't run the regular washer either." She answered her own question. "No, of course you can't." She put back her shoulders. "Maybe I'll go comb my hair."

At least she didn't say things like *I must look a fright.*

A half bath was off the entrance hall. Matt went to set the oven timer.

When he turned back, Daisy was standing in the doorway. From her dazed expression, he knew she had seen herself in the mirror. *I look a fright.* He waited for it.

A laugh started somewhere deep in her belly, then

began to escape in short gasps. "Sorry," she choked as she headed out the side door. "I really don't want the cake to fall."

That set off both of them. Quickly he followed her outside, holding in his own bellow of laughter until they were safely on the grass. He'd never seen a woman laugh like that.

"Is it okay if I use your shower?" Daisy asked when they were able to stop.

"Sure." Then he remembered. "We're out of towels."

Lordy lordy, Jack Snow's forty.

If anybody in town didn't know Jack's age already, they found out when they walked into the café the next morning. Ron and the others had hung a big banner on one wall. The same message was lettered on the sign outside the Shell station. Also, someone had put a notice in the *Potts Gazette.*

Supposedly they were only having a small, quiet celebration at home, but Daisy had arranged a full-fledged surprise party.

Anyway, a lot of people came, and even though Jack got three mugs that said he was over the hill, he didn't act like he particularly agreed. He really liked the new stereo headphones that Matt bought for him. "Isn't this expensive?" he asked. He didn't wait for Matt's answer because Daisy was insisting that he had to wear his pointed birthday hat while a man with a camera snapped a picture of him with his arm around her.

The only bad thing that happened was that just as they were cutting the cake, the phone rang for Daisy. So she couldn't even stay for her own cake.

She had brought her uniform, just in case. She changed quickly. "Save a piece for me," she called as she left. "I'll come back later if I can."

Jack followed her to the door. Matt was standing close enough that he couldn't help seeing them kiss. "I'll see you later, then," Jack said to her as she went out the door.

She turned. "It could be a lot later."

He nodded. "Then I'll see you a lot later."

Jack returned to his party.

MATT FIGURED THAT Daisy must have come in really late when he woke up around two and heard them talking downstairs.

Daisy sounded tired and depressed. Matt had to go to the bathroom, so he heard some of what they were talking about. "Oh, lord, there was this little girl and she didn't know what was happening except that her daddy was beating on her mama and I was supposed to fix things. Sure, I can take her father away this time. Her mother will get a restraining order. I know perfectly well that woman is going to let him come back and he'll be nice for a while until he has something to drink or she burns the eggs."

"Maybe not," Jack said. "Don't you think that you're making an impression, too?"

"I don't know. Maybe I don't come across as a woman."

"Honey, trust me. In or out of uniform, you come across as a woman." There was a silence, and Matt was about to return to bed.

"Don't try to make me feel better, Jack Snow," she told him crossly. "I couldn't even bake a cake without your son's help."

Matt decided to stick around in case she was going to say nice things about him.

His dad spoke. "Everybody said the cake was great. I saved some for you."

"Real women bake cakes. And cookies. Without help." Daisy sighed. "Matt actually knows how to cook, doesn't he?" She sounded accusing.

"He learned at his father's knee."

"I'm amazed that he didn't laugh in my face." She groaned. "I can't believe this. I'm a sexist pig."

Jack laughed. "In this house we'd say that you were a sexist officer of the law. But you're learning."

Then Daisy was laughing, too. "I didn't mean it that way." She stopped. "Sometimes I don't think I even have any maternal instincts. Really."

Matt froze.

"You get along all right with my kid," Jack said.

"Your son is easy to get along with. He's easygoing, like his old man. He's going to be another charmer, too." Another sigh. "I've never gone all gooshy when I see babies. I enjoy taking care of my sister's kids, but I've never minded handing them back. See? No maternal instincts. Not one."

"You're just feeling down," Jack soothed.

Matt went to bed, but he lay there a long time, thinking. At school he knew a guy in a foster home. He'd been placed there because his mother married somebody who didn't want kids. Matt had always figured that if Jack remarried, it would be like somebody else coming to live with the two of them. Someone would be sleeping in Jack's room with him and sharing their things.

He never thought of the possibility that he might not fit into their lives.

If nothing else, he wouldn't end up in a foster home. He wouldn't live with his grandmother, either.

He had money.

CHAPTER
12

MONEY.

They were earning it while they worked for Dermot, all right. Matt was perspiring. He was dirty. He was scratched. Mosquitoes dive-bombed him, scouting out the blood beaded on his bare arms and back. His jeans protected the rest of him, but not entirely. He'd packed deep-woods repellent before heading over to Dermot's that morning, the greasy kind that stank of garlic. He and Lewis slathered on plenty, but these mosquitoes were either mutants or salad-lovers. If it wasn't for the sand sticking to his sweat, Matt figured that by now they'd have more of his blood than he did.

As he slashed down more and more prickle bushes on Dermot's property, Matt fell into an even rhythm that was almost hypnotic. He felt completely alone, like the prince working his way to Sleeping Beauty's castle.

He wasn't. Lewis was working over to his right. They kept a deliberate distance. If they were really close to each other, they'd probably slash each other along with the blackberry vines. He couldn't see Lewis as he worked, but he could sure hear him going through his litany of English and Chinese swear words.

Dermot came out of his shack. "Do you boys want something to drink yet?"

"Yeah!" Matt yelled. He carried the machete with him and laid it carefully by a tree. He'd made a mistake the first day by throwing it down where he stood. It had taken him almost an hour to locate it in the thorny vines.

Lewis didn't look a whole lot better than he did as they walked down to the house, drawing off their gloves. He'd had his new glasses for a week, but he wore the old ones while he worked. Neither had on a shirt because it was so hot. If their tans had faded during the time they worked for Wong, they'd gained back that color and more.

"I hope you two are thirsty." They grunted as they threw themselves down on the porch. Dermot had mixed some lemonade in an old pickle jar, which he brought out with two mugs. "Sorry there's no ice, but you know how it is." Dermot had an old-type fridge with round corners. It didn't make ice.

The lemonade went down okay. Matt's hands shook from weariness, and part of the liquid spilled down his chin and onto his chest. Lewis wasn't faring much better.

It was three. They'd been working since eight that morning.

This was their fourth day of cutting down prickle bushes and moving rocks. Those were the tasks that Dermot had set for them.

That's what they were paying him for.

Dermot kept a single wooden chair on the porch. He sat with his feet on the railing, drinking beer from a bottle. The two boys occupied the wooden steps and dribbled lemonade on themselves. "I think it's getting hotter," he said.

They didn't have to be told that. When they started working on Monday, there were clouds overhead, even a few drops of rain now and then.

Dermot continued. "The radio says we're in for a scorcher the next couple of days."

Matt was too tired to groan.

"I don't want the two of you on my hands with sunstroke. So maybe you'd better take a couple of days off until there's a break. Everything here can wait."

Neither boy said anything. Neither moved.

"Besides, I'm not used to all this company. The truth is that I keep feeling like I have to entertain you. Like I should bring out potato chips, that kind of thing."

Their skin was caked with ocean salt and garlic oil. Matt figured that they *were* potato chips.

"We're not asking you to entertain us," Lewis said.

"Or feed us," Matt added. They brought their own

lunches, although for the past two days they'd been too tired to eat them.

Dermot rose. "Boys, I'm setting you free. Go enjoy your summer for a few days. You won't have many summers left that you can call your own." He stretched and headed toward the door. "I'm going to contribute to our culture by writing poetry."

They remained sitting there. They had paid Dermot the first five thousand dollars on the day they started working for him. The next day he went into the city to talk to a man about printing up his poetry for him. He returned that evening, bubbling over about binding and paper quality and other things that went straight over Matt's head. He also brought cases of beer for himself and pop for them.

Lewis' mom called Dermot a thoughtful employer. Matt figured he'd probably do the same for any dumb animals, so they wouldn't die on him.

Besides, Lewis' mom wasn't there when Dermot ceremoniously presented them with receipts for the pop.

FINALLY THEY STOOD and laid their mugs on the porch. Silently they cleaned their machetes and put them in the tool shed. Silently they headed toward their bikes.

As he gripped the handlebars, Matt's hands stung from the blisters on his palms. Neither boy had thought of bringing gloves the first day. They stood there with their bikes while the sun baked them into garlic-flavored, heavily salted, extra-crispy human potato chips.

"Lew," Matt said. "Does it ever seem to you like this money owns us? Like maybe it isn't worth it?"

"It is to me."

They'd already told Dermot that at summer's end he was going to give them computers as a bonus for hard work. They could tell the poet didn't like that idea. (*Generous, ain't I? I don't like the smell of this. Every charity on the coast is likely to come after me.*)

As they started walking their bikes up the road, Matt's muscles ached. "This is really messing up our summer."

"Think winter," Lewis said. "Think computer. Hey, you were the one who kept saying we needed money and we needed jobs."

Matt stopped dead. "I meant I wanted an extra twenty sometimes. This isn't a whole lot of fun."

Lewis' eyes narrowed. "I don't need fun. I need that computer. I need a bike."

Matt bit his tongue to keep from responding. Lewis hadn't needed a computer when he didn't have a chance of getting one. He made do with his crappy bike.

As they hit the main road, Matt wasn't sure why he and Lewis were mad at each other, but they definitely were. He tried to lighten things up. "So, what do you want to do for the next couple of days? Laze around in the sun?"

To his surprise, Lewis agreed.

THREE DAYS LATER, Matt was lying on his beach towel at Joneson Park, not thinking about work. Not thinking about money. Thinking about the sunshine, which was free.

Upper Potts didn't have a very large beach, and it seemed like he knew almost everybody there. Lewis lay on another towel next to his, maybe sleeping, maybe not. All around the beach lay girls on beach towels. Maybe most of them didn't have bodies like he'd seen on TV, but then, neither did the guys. Sometimes Matt wondered where all the people lived that he saw on TV, like maybe there was a Prettytown somewhere and the rest of the people lived in the Uglies.

He dug his watch out of his pack. Dermot had phoned the night before to say he'd pick them up that afternoon. Lewis raised his head groggily. "We have another hour," Matt told him.

The other boy groaned. "He's probably going to have us moving rocks again."

"Probably."

Lewis began to sink down again. He stopped. "To the right," he whispered. "Strawberry pink bikini."

Matt glanced over. A girl with long black hair lay on her stomach, face cradled in her arms, while a blond guy who looked seventeen or so smoothed suntan lotion on her bare back. "Not bad." Pretty good, actually. Golden skin, curves. "Since when do you look at that kind of thing?"

"I look." Lewis paused. "What I mean is, that's Sara. I think that's her boyfriend with her. He looks like the guy in the picture."

The spot where they'd spread their towels seemed entirely too close for comfort. "Jeez," Matt said. "Don't wave at her."

"Why not?"

"Don't wave."

Sara's voice cut into his head. "Hey, Matt," she called from her towel. "Aren't you talking to me?"

He turned slightly in her direction. "Hi." The greeting came out muffled. Through his sunglasses, he saw her watching him through her sunglasses. He thought she looked puzzled. The guy with her said something. She tossed her hair back and laughed.

Obviously she'd forgotten about him already.

"Let's see how the water is." He left his sunglasses in the pack and ran toward the waves.

Cold was how it was. Matt gasped as the water hit his skin. He immersed himself completely, and came up with a squashed beer can. "This is disgusting," he said aloud, but Lewis was nowhere to be seen. He caught sight of him talking to a boy from their class.

He hadn't thought about it, but ever since they'd found the money, Lewis was the only other person he'd seen. Maybe Lewis was his closest friend, but he wasn't his only friend. The money made them spend all their time together.

He swam around for a while. Good stuff. He glanced toward the beach, toward where Sara Lee was lying. She was sitting up, combing her hair. Shaking her head about something.

He wasn't there to think about Sara Lee.

Lots of little kids were on the beach, most of them wearing big hats. Little kids with buckets and shovels, and ladies in bathing suits that sagged and bulged, and guys with beer bellies, and guys with muscles, throwing Frisbees around to impress the girls who didn't sag and bulge.

Matt spotted a guy from his class who was with his sister from the next grade down. They both splashed water on the girl while she shrieked in mock pain. She splashed them back, giving them as good as she got. Matt dove under the water while her brother diverted her attention. He was about to tackle her from behind when she hit him in the nose with her elbow.

"Oh, my gosh, I'm sorry." She looked dazed as he rose from the water, howling with laughter.

"She got your nose, man," the other boy said.

Matt wiped his nose on the back of his hand and it

came away blood-streaked. That made him laugh harder, which made his nose bleed harder.

The girl was looking around. "A tissue . . ."

"We're in the water," the boy pointed out. "What's he supposed to do with a tissue in the water?"

"No problem," Matt said. If he had a hundred-dollar bill, he bet it wouldn't dissolve. Money was indestructible. He pinched his nostrils together. "No problem," he repeated except that his words came out sounding funny.

The girl smiled. She was okay-looking for thirteen.

Matt headed in toward his towel.

The girl came with him, hitching up her suit. "You're positive that you're all right?"

He took his fingers away. "The bleeding is stopping." He pinched his nostrils again, more gently.

She seemed to be waiting for something.

"See you," Matt said as he turned away.

He thought she looked disappointed. "See you."

As he headed toward the towel, he spotted Lewis sitting on Sara's towel with Sara and her boyfriend. Lewis had his book with him. He looked like he was giving them the standard lecture about whether orcs and goblins were the same thing. Sara seemed interested, but the guy with her looked bored.

Good stuff. Not that Matt cared. He threw himself down on his towel, grabbing up his shirt to use as a handkerchief in case his nose started bleeding again. Lewis' shadow fell across him.

"What happened to you?" Lewis asked.

"We were messing around in the water. A girl got me with her elbow." Girls were ferocious. "So, how's Sara doing?"

"She's okay. She asked how you were doing. I told her you were okay."

"Great." Matt leaned back. "Everybody's okay."

Lewis dug his watch out of his pack. "Dermot's coming around in another half hour."

Matt dozed for a while. He awoke briefly when he heard Sara say loudly, *"Don't!"*

He wasn't the only one who looked up. Sara was sitting up on the towel, adjusting her top. She was laughing, but she looked annoyed, too. The guy she was with certainly didn't look happy. She put her hand on his briefly, as if she was apologizing. Her friend stood up and headed across the beach toward the concession stand near the road.

Matt felt like Sara was looking at him. That was the problem with sunglasses. You could never be sure about anything.

The sun had risen as high as it was going to. "Another twenty minutes," Lewis said. Then, "another ten minutes."

Like there was some reason for him to count down.

Like they were bombs set to explode.

Matt felt groggy when he sat up and started to put his clothes over his damp suit. Sand stuck to his feet, and he had to brush them off before he could put on his shoes. He touched his nose tentatively. "Any blood?" he asked.

Lewis examined him. "Nothing obvious."

They spotted the van parked outside the government liquor store and headed that way. Dermot was coming toward it, carrying a couple of wine bottles in a paper bag.

"Did you two get enough of a rest?" he asked when Matt slid open the side door. The bottles clanked as he set them inside.

Lewis scrambled in. "Not bad. What's on the agenda today?"

"Agenda." The old man scratched his beard. "I'll have to consult my personal secretary about that, see if I have such a thing as an agenda around the place."

"An agenda," Lewis said. "It's like a schedule."

"Ah." Dermot nodded. "I see. Well, there are things that need fixing."

Matt was about to get in when a sudden blur of movement passed him. He turned to see Sara Lee climbing in next to Lewis. She wore shorts and an open shirt over her bathing suit. "So," she said pleasantly, "where are we going?"

"We?" Lewis looked as surprised as he was.

Dermot was frowning. "Young lady, these two boys work for me. Unless something has changed, you don't."

"I can help." She held up her arm and clenched her fist to make a muscle. "I'm strong, see?" She nodded toward Matt. "Lewis says you fix things and stuff like that. Hey, I'm bored."

Matt glanced back at the beach. He spotted the guy she had been sitting with. He had an ice cream bar in each hand, and he was looking around wildly. She'd run out on him.

Matt tasted blood. "What about the guy you were with?"

She shrugged. "He's too—" She stopped, obviously uncomfortable. "He's too friendly."

"He's your boyfriend, right?"

"I guess." She curled her hair around her finger, her eyes sad. "He's camping on the beach—like he's doing me a big favor, you know? Things just don't seem the same here. We don't have a lot to talk about." She brightened when she saw the book Lewis was holding. "Can I borrow that when you're finished?"

Dermot motioned Matt away from the van. In a low voice he asked, "Does she know . . . ?"

Matt shook his head. Abruptly he grinned. "No

harm if she comes along for the afternoon, right?" he asked loudly.

Lewis looked perplexed.

Matt took the front seat. "Belt up," he called back to Sara. "If you want to help, you can help."

Dermot started to pull out. "I hope you kids realize that you're destroying my reputation as a hermit."

"A hermit crab," Sara said primly. "That's what I heard."

Dermot grunted. "You heard right."

Matt watched in the rearview mirror as Sara smoothed her hair between her fingers. She smiled. "A hermit crab who writes poetry." She looked around. "So, what are we doing today?"

"Nothing very exciting." Matt spoke casually. "Have you ever moved an outhouse?"

Behind him, Lewis caught his breath. Dermot grimaced.

"What's an outhouse?" Sara asked curiously. "Something like a toolshed?"

Dermot cleared his throat. "You can tell it from the toolshed because of the crescent moon carved in the door." He slowed to let ferry traffic go by.

"Uh, Matt—" Lewis began.

"This is as good a day for the job as any."

"Sure," Sara said. "Why not? I can help move an outhouse. It's not very heavy, is it?"

"Shouldn't be." Dermot's voice was cheerful as he

spoke to Matt. "I gather that you want to leave a lasting impression with this girl."

That was just what he wanted to do.

Money wasn't the only thing that could buy revenge.

To give her credit, Sara Lee was a good sport. They couldn't really move the outhouse because first they had to dig a hole. But she wasn't expected to know that. "A bathroom?" she cried when Dermot suggested she open the door and look inside. "A bathroom? Outside?"

"City girl," Dermot mumbled.

She was holding her nose. "Where is—It doesn't flush. Then where does—" Matt could see that she was getting the idea. "Oh."

"You offered to help," he pointed out silkily.

She thought about it for a minute. Then she folded her arms. "Okay."

"The girl is offering to shovel crap with you," Dermot observed. "You're not likely to find a more sincere offer of friendship."

"Maybe we should find something else to do," Matt said after a moment.

Lewis looked relieved.

She helped prepare Dermot's fence for painting.

The old man was pleasant enough, but he called Matt over after she'd been working awhile. "I don't want to hurt your friend's feelings," he said, "but I don't want you to bring her here again. Or anybody else. I wasn't planning on opening a teen hangout."

Also, Sara was intelligent enough that she might figure out what was happening, or one of them might make an offhand remark about the money. He and Lewis conferred. They agreed they'd be better off if they didn't hang around Sara at all.

AFTER THAT, THINGS returned to normal, at least for a few days. They sanded and hammered and painted. They bagged bottles for Dermot to haul off. Their blisters toughened into calluses, their skin into leather. If somebody handed them rifles, they could say they were going through training for a desert war.

They didn't move the outhouse, but they painted it. "We need a vacation," Matt said as they cleaned off their brushes in a jar of turpentine.

"This is our vacation. Anyway, we just had three days off."

An idea began to grow and thrive in Matt's brain like a worm in a particularly juicy apple. He almost dropped the brush. "We need to go somewhere, some-where we've always wanted to go. Somewhere that money can take us and we won't have to be away more than a few days."

They stared at each other. Both formed the magic word at the same time. "Disneyland!"

AN ADULT HAD to make the arrangements, of course. Dermot already had plans to head into the city to see about his book. While there, he agreed to visit a travel agent's office. He rubbed his thumb against his middle finger. "Let's have some cash for the travel agent."

Matt bit his lip. "How much do you think it will cost?"

Dermot reached over to pick up a newspaper, then flipped through the ads. He stabbed at a section. "This should give you an idea." He walked back into the house and a moment later Matt heard the fridge door opening.

Lewis studied the paper. "Okay," he said finally. "The family rate looks best." He glanced at Matt. "Maybe you should hand over a thou tomorrow."

"Family?" Matt's eyes widened.

"Us," Lewis said succinctly. "Us and our grandfather."

Dermot was standing in the doorway with a bottle of beer. He looked around, then pointed to himself questioningly.

Lewis nodded. Dermot shuddered.

The old man took a long drink. "California," he said at last. "Sure. Why the hell not?"

THE NEXT THING they had to do was ask permission from their parents to go away for a few days.

Lewis figured that one out. No sweat.

That was easy for him to say. In Lewis' little house, a person absent meant breathing room. Jack needed Matt for company. Matt would be missed.

They agreed that Lewis would ask permission first.

Like he said, no sweat. "Mom said to pack clean underwear," he said on the phone. "Your turn."

Matt didn't have a whole lot of practice lying to his father. Keeping secrets, sure, but not face-on, bald lying. "After he gets home tonight."

WHEN JACK CAME into the house that afternoon, Daisy was with him. Matt wasn't about to say anything in front of her, so he waited until she left the room. His hands were perspiring.

"Dad?"

Jack was wiping off the kitchen counter. "Do you think you could clean up after yourself when you make a sandwich? This place looks like you've been strewing crumbs for pigeons."

"Sorry. But, see, Dad, Lewis and I were talking. There's this guy who moved to Vancouver. Keith. You remember Keith?"

Jack nodded.

"Anyway, we ran into him when we were at Play-land. And he said that Lewis and I should come and spend a couple of days at his place. Three days, I mean."

Daisy had returned. She stood very still in the doorway.

"I was wondering if that would be okay."

Jack was looking at Daisy. "Three days," he said.

"Actually," Matt went on, "we'd leave on Tuesday afternoon and come back Saturday."

"Four nights," Daisy said.

Jack didn't stop looking at her even though he was talking to Matt. His gaze drifted to Matt. "I'm assuming that this boy's parents will be there."

"We'll have an adult with us at all times." At least that wasn't a lie.

"Sounds good." Maybe Jack was staring at Daisy, but Daisy was glancing at him and then at the floor. And then she and his dad were both taking each other in. To Matt they looked like they were both starving to death.

"So, can I go?" Matt asked. He was getting the uncomfortable feeling that his request had been forgotten.

Jack nodded. "It's fine with me."

"Have a wonderful time," Daisy said.

Jack was grinning at her. "Remember to say please and thank you. And pack clean underwear."

They could go! Matt wished that his father wouldn't mention underwear in front of Daisy, but the main thing was that he'd been given permission. "So it's really okay?"

Jack turned toward him, his eyes warm. "It's really okay. Maybe I can even come up with some extra spending money for you."

"I have enough cash." Matt mumbled the words.

His dad smiled. "That's something I thought I'd never hear. My kid's getting older."

"TWO THOUSAND MILES," Matt said as he looked at the travel material Dermot had picked up. "How far is that?"

Lewis computed the figures on his calculator. "Three thousand, two hundred eighteen kilometers. That's both ways."

They were flying out of Seattle rather than Vancouver. Less chance that way of running into anyone they knew, Dermot said. Also cheaper.

In miles or kilometers, they were going a long way.

TUESDAY MORNING CAME, as usual. Jack left for the café, also as usual. Dermot picked up Lewis and Matt in the van. They headed south, almost too keyed up to argue about which radio station to play. Not usual.

The old man hardly said anything. "Did you bring

your birth certificates?" was all he asked. Both nodded. Dermot didn't seem to care whether or not they brought extra underwear.

FIVE HOURS LATER, they arrived at SeaTac Airport. Inside, both boys headed for the big window overlooking the landing area. They watched the planes land and take off. After another wait in a smaller room, they clambered aboard one of the airplanes they'd seen below. "This is great," Matt called over his shoulder when they were all inside. Airplanes smelled great, like they were filled with artificial air.

"Great," Lewis mumbled. His face looked green.

Matt suddenly realized something. Maybe he hadn't been on a plane since the last time he visited his grandmother, but Lewis had never been on one at all. "Planes are cool," Matt said as they took their seats. Dermot had a seat by the window, but he said he'd rather be on the aisle. He traded with Lewis.

"Man, oh man." The plane began to take off. Lewis squeezed his eyes shut tight.

He was missing the best part. "Take a look," Matt said. "No kidding."

Lewis opened one eye slightly. Then he sat there staring out the window at the clouds coming to meet them and the ground receding below. Like it was a movie. "I've seen pictures," he whispered when the seat belt sign turned off. "Only, I never thought it would be this good."

Later, a steward came down the aisle with a trolley. He served a drink to Dermot and ginger ale to the boys. Tiny sacks of salted peanuts, too. Lewis stuck his unopened pack into his shirt pocket. Matt polished off his in one mouthful. Dermot stopped the steward on his way back up the aisle. "These are growing boys," he said. "Do you think they might have some more of those peanuts?"

Another sack of peanuts went into Lewis' pocket, plus one that Dermot gave him. Matt eyed him, puzzled. It was like when they found the money and Lewis still insisted on picking up empty bottles. He leaned closer. "You look like a lopsided girl."

Lewis elbowed him. "So maybe I'll get hungry later."

So okay.

EVEN MATT WASN'T prepared for the sheer expanse that was Los Angeles. It went on forever under the hazy heat. As the plane began to descend, he looked down on rows of swimming pools in all shapes. At the tops of palm trees—he'd only seen palm trees on TV. Highways snaked in every direction, filled with cars that glittered under the late afternoon sunlight.

He had brought along a few sticks of Juicy Fruit so

they could chew gum while they were landing. Jack had once told him that chewing would keep down the pressure in his ears. He didn't want to think about Jack. If Jack knew where he was, he'd go ballistic.

Lewis watched everything when they landed. As the plane taxied to a halt, he grinned at Matt. "We're in California."

Duh.

His voice rose. "We made it."

Double duh. Abruptly Matt realized that he had swallowed his gum.

"Don't leave anything behind," Dermot said as he stood.

THE FAMILY TRAVEL package included a rented tan sedan. They drove to a pizza house, but both boys were almost too hyper to eat. Almost. Then both ran down like old watches.

They were yawning at the motel registration desk. "Stay alert, boys," Dermot ordered. "I'm not planning to tuck you in."

"Yes, Grandpa," Lewis spoke up.

Dermot stiffened and harrumphed before signing his name in the registration book.

THE NEXT MORNING, they arrived at Disneyland before opening time. Mobs of people were already waiting in front of the ticket booths. The snow-capped peak of the Matterhorn gleamed before Matt, beckoning him. He was about to join the crowd when he became aware that Lewis had stopped. "Come on!" he yelled.

Lewis was staring up at the monorail and over at the gardens. Not moving. He looked back toward the parking area.

Great. They'd made it to Disneyland and now Lewis was acting like an old dog that expected to be tied outside the market. Matt butted him impatiently with his shoulder. "Move it."

Dermot lit his pipe. "You've got one-day passes," he pointed out. "You might as well use 'em."

They stayed with the main crowd as Lewis allowed himself to be swept through Main Street. They emerged in the plaza facing Sleeping Beauty's castle, then stopped to read the signs. "Let's go to Frontierland first," Matt said. Lewis just nodded.

It wasn't until they were careening around the curves of the Big Thunder Mountain Railroad, holding on for their lives, that he came out of his daze. "Matt," Lewis shouted over the shrieks of the other passengers. "This is what it's for—the money."

The money was for fun. "Yeah!"

THEY SAW EVERYTHING they wanted, but it took all day. Dermot didn't go on every ride with them, preferring to sit and write in his red notebook. Space Mountain was Matt's favorite. He spent a lot of time in line waiting to ride Space Mountain. That and Pirate's Cove.

They stayed until the fireworks, then afterward they went to a Mexican restaurant for a late dinner. They were just leaving when they passed a guy asking for change. Lewis gave him a few coins, plus the sacks of peanuts from his pocket. When he rejoined Matt and Dermot, he was whistling.

"Today was good," Lewis said.

Universal Studios the next day was good, too. It wasn't like Disneyland, but Matt saw all the shows and he was never bored. Just as he had at Disneyland, Lewis took a lot of pictures. They handed the camera to a Japanese tourist so he could take pictures of them together with their "grandfather."

After the shoot-out in the western town, Dermot started scribbling again. When Matt told him that he and Lewis were taking the tram tour a second time, he just grunted. "Imagine," he said. "Imagine that you spend your entire life dying, then getting up. Falling and rising. How do you know when you're dead?"

You don't get up again. Matt figured that out right off.

When you were dead, you were dead.

FOR THE THIRD day they all went on the roller coasters at Magic Mountain. "Another day," Matt groaned when they reached the motel. "We need one more day. We didn't get to Knott's Berry Farm."

Dermot regarded him slant-eyed. "The last thing I need is another day baby-sitting you tykes."

"We have to go back," Lewis said practically. "If we aren't on time, somebody might decide to call Keith's place."

True. One thing that bugged Matt was that he couldn't buy souvenirs. Okay, he *could,* but he wouldn't dare show them off.

Everything was reversed going back, like rewinding a tape. At the L.A. Airport, Matt was sure he spotted a girl from Potts, and he started sweating. It wasn't her. Then Lewis grabbed his arm as they were boarding the plane. His voice shook. "It's Mr. Norton. He's in line behind us."

Their band teacher. Matt almost fell. "Where?"

Lewis punched him in the shoulder. "Gotcha!"

"Boys," Dermot said sternly. "No fighting."

At SeaTac they collected the van and drove north. They presented their birth certificates at the border. Lewis held his breath until the customs officer waved them through. Matt exhaled at the same time. He thought Dermot did, too.

It wasn't until he was on the ferry heading home that he relaxed. The whole thing was beginning to feel almost normal.

Seagulls wheeled overhead. "You know what?" Lewis said as they pulled into the dock. "Potts is small."

Dermot laughed. "Just figured that out, did you?"

As he let himself into the house, Matt half expected to find his dad waiting for him, furious. *"I called your friend Keith. He said he hasn't seen you in months. You boys have some tall explaining to do."*

"Uh . . . well, see, we found this money."

"Found? You found money?"

Jack was waiting, all right. But he wasn't mad. In fact, he looked almost embarrassed.

"Did you have a good time?" he asked.

"Sure." Before they parted company, Matt and Lewis prepared a story about the things they did while visiting Keith. "On Wednesday we went to Playland and—"

"I'm getting married," Jack interrupted. For a second, it seemed like Matt couldn't breathe. Jack looked up at the ceiling and then down at the floor. "To Daisy." Like Matt was surprised. Like he was hearing the announcement from a stranger about two people he didn't know very well. Jack swallowed. "We're getting married. To each other."

Matt started beaming. "No kidding?"

His father laughed. "No kidding."

"Like when?" This was good. This was so good. He wanted to run to the phone, to call Lewis. Then he thought of something else that was really important, so important that at first he couldn't ask. "Dad? Where am I going to live?"

"Sorry?" Jack was standing there grinning, but that seemed to bring him around. "Where do you live when? What are you talking about?"

"When you get married, do I keep living here?" Maybe he and Lewis could get an apartment. That would probably be okay. No, wait. If he and Lewis got an apartment, then they'd have to explain why they had money to rent an apartment.

Jack still hadn't answered. "Why wouldn't you keep living here?" he asked at last.

"Maybe you—maybe Daisy—" He swallowed. "I don't know." He was beginning to feel uncomfortable. "Maybe you wouldn't want me around anymore, okay?"

Jack grabbed his shoulders so hard that Matt winced. "I want you around," he said. "Right now I'm enriching my life. I'm not letting go of the good stuff I already have. You're part of the good stuff. You'll leave some day, when it's time. But not until then. Is that clear?"

"Clear," Matt managed.

"I don't want you to tell Daisy that you were thinking something like that. She's been talking about things the three of us can do together, day trips and things like that. Camping."

If Matt knew one thing, it was that his dad was not a camper. "We're going camping?"

"It might happen, sometime. After the honeymoon." Jack straightened. "Speaking of which, the wedding is in three weeks. You're best man, if you want to be."

If he wanted to be. All Matt knew about being best man was what he'd seen on TV, a guy handing over a ring to a nervous bridegroom. "Okay." Something struck him. "Three weeks?"

"Daisy has holiday time scheduled. Also, we both want to hold the reception in the garden, which means warm weather."

"Here?" Matt wouldn't exactly call their fenced backyard a garden, despite the rosebushes growing around the edges.

His father nodded. "The main thing is that for a few days, we're going to have hot and cold running relatives in town."

That was okay. Matt didn't often see his cousins.

"Your grandmother will stay at the house before the wedding and while we're away on our honeymoon." He cleared his throat. "I'm afraid you'll have to give up your room temporarily."

Matt stared. "My room?"

"It can't be that bad." Jack chuckled. "Or maybe it can. Tell you what. I'll give you a hand shoveling it out."

"No, thanks," Matt managed. He had heard that when you were drowning, your life flashed before your eyes.

Instead, the things he'd bought over the past few weeks flashed through his mind. His room was packed with them, the best that money could buy.

Computers.

Stereo equipment.

Electronic games.

He was a dead man.

CHAPTER
14

WHEN THEY TOLD DERMOT THE NEWS, HIS FIRST RESPONSE was to laugh. That was also his second response, after they said they wanted to store the computers and stuff at his place. "Look around you," he said. "Do you see a lot of spare room?"

The entire house was no larger than Matt's bedroom. "It would only be for a few weeks," Matt pleaded miserably. "Until Dad and Daisy come back from their honeymoon."

"We'll pay you," Lewis said.

For a second Matt thought the old man was going to get mad. Then he shrugged. "The company putting out my book showed me different types of covers I can have. So maybe there's a kind I prefer that costs a little more."

They settled on a price.

"By the way," Dermot asked casually. "What are you two planning to do with the cash?"

Both boys groaned.

———

"MY ROOM!" MATT exclaimed to Lewis. "It's got all this—*room*."

It was one week before the wedding. The last of the boxes had been packed into the van and transferred into Dermot's shack. Now there was nothing to do but clean up.

Lewis fished a paper airplane out from behind the radiator. A good thing. If Matt's grandmother had an eagle eye for specks of dust, she wasn't about to miss a folded hundred-dollar bill.

Lewis just stood there holding the airplane. "Do you want us to get caught? It's bad enough that your dad is marrying a cop."

"My dad," Matt said between clenched teeth, "is marrying Daisy. *Daisy* is going to be my stepmother, not a cop."

"What's the difference?"

"Lots." Matt gulped. "There's a lot of difference."

Lewis sat down on the bed with a glum expression. "When she moves in, what are we supposed to do? We can't bring the things back here. She's bound to smell that something is wrong."

"We could turn in the rest of the money."

Lewis's head went up sharply. "Oh, sure. Right."

"We already have everything we want. Last time we were in town, we couldn't even find anything else to buy."

"Nothing that would fit in here." Lewis paused. "You sound like we'd be allowed to keep the stuff we have."

"Wouldn't we?" Matt hadn't thought about that.

"Okay," Lewis said. "Suppose we tell your stepmother the Mountie that we found a suitcase of money six weeks ago. And, oh, yeah, we've been spending it. And, oh, yeah, we have an adult working for us."

"Disneyland," Matt whispered. His dad would have a fit if he learned about that.

"Right." Now Lewis was up and pacing. "Disneyland. Okay, let's look at what would happen to us."

"Nothing would happen," Matt said. "It's not like we stole it or anything."

"Okay." Lewis was on a roll. "First our parents kill us or ground us for life or whatever. Then everybody hears about it. So half of everybody figures we shouldn't have spent anything. The other half figures we're complete idiots for giving anything back. We're celebrities both ways."

"We could keep a few thousand," Matt suggested. "We don't have to return it all." He paused. "Hey, Lew, I'm happy about this wedding. I'm going to be my dad's best man." He had tried on his suit recently for the first time in a year. After taking a look at his protruding ankles and wrists, Jack took him into the city to buy a new one.

Lewis snorted. "The best man at a cop wedding has a suitcase full of drug money. Great."

Matt was getting choked with all the talk of cops, like it was us and them. "You wanted to turn in the suitcase when we found it, remember? Remember the little old lady who lost her life savings?"

Lewis snorted.

"We have what we want. If the rest of this money is going to get us in trouble, we don't need it anymore."

"Speak for yourself!" Lewis yelled. "You've always had everything."

They stared at each other.

Lewis' voice lowered. "I never in my whole life had a new bike. Not once. You always did."

"I didn't know it bugged you."

"Yeah," Lewis said. He began looking around the room again, searching for any evidence left behind. "Well, neither did I."

GERRY WAS CLEANING his gun in a small hotel room in Vancouver with a not-so-scenic view of the back of a dry cleaning establishment. He was a slim man with a mustache he kept trimmed like that guy on TV, Geraldo Rivera. He looked up when his partner came in carrying a bulging paper sack from an organic food store. Ed was more the Schwarzenegger type.

"I got a call an hour ago," Gerry said. "About Charlie Swenson."

"Where did he turn up?"

"Some place up on the coast. Dead."

"Charlie?" Ed gaped. "Who got him?"

"It was his heart."

"Aw, jeez. Charlie." Ed sat down heavily on the bed. "Last Christmas he played Santa Claus for my sister's kids."

Gerry looked bored. "Maybe you're forgetting something? Like we were supposed to *take care* of him."

"Well, yeah. But he was a real good Santa Claus. The kids were nuts about him." He barely registered Gerry's open suitcase on the bed. "I would've had a lot of trouble killing him. I mean, hurting him, okay. I could hurt him, like, as a warning. Break his arm or leg or something. The collarbone—that hurts. What about you? Could you have killed old Charlie?"

"I just follow orders," Gerry said coolly. "Nothing personal. Charlie would've understood that. He was a professional." He sighted the gun at an imaginary target and pretended to shoot, then set it down again. "You better not say things like that where anybody can hear you. Otherwise you're likely to find yourself back where you started."

Ed shuddered. He had started out collecting bad debts for a loan shark. This was definitely a step up for him. Gerry figured it right that he didn't want to go back.

"I would have killed him," he said evenly, "if it came to that."

"Anyway, it looks like he made an unscheduled side trip to some place called Potts. His daughter used to live there. Guess what?"

"What?"

"She's been a nun in Toronto for the last three years. She never heard from him. She's going to pray for his soul."

"That's good, right?" Ed took an apple from the bag. "I never figured he ran off with the cash." He noticed Gerry removing shirts from the bureau drawer. "What are you doing?"

"Oh, yeah," Gerry said. "I guess I didn't tell you. We're supposed to take care of any loose ends." He examined two ties, put one into his suitcase. "Unless Charlie dropped the suitcase into the ocean before he died, it's a fair bet that somebody has the money." He folded extra clips of ammunition into his socks. "Enough time has passed for that somebody to get careless."

15

"That's the way the money goes.
POP goes the weasel."

AT *POP*, JOEY GIGGLED WILDLY. MATT LAUGHED WITH
him.

They were at Lewis' house. Matt was playing with
the baby on Lewis' bed while Lewis finished taping up
the bottom of the crib mattress. Which was where they
had decided to put the money until things cooled down.

"What about when they change the kid's sheets?"
Matt asked worriedly. It hadn't escaped his notice that
Joey wet his diaper an awful lot. There was definitely
an overflow factor. He didn't like to say so, but every
time he walked into Lewis' room, he felt like he was
breathing in a cloud of warm pee.

"Look at the way the sheet fits onto the mattress,"
Lewis reassured him. "Corinne never flips it over. And
even if she did . . ."

Matt saw what he meant. The crib was old-fashioned with a thick mattress, bought at a garage sale.

The mattress cover was blue plastic and ripped. Nobody was going to notice more tape.

"Mo-mo-mo-*money*." Joey laughed.

"Corinne thinks he's saying Mommy," Lewis said as he slid the mattress back into the crib. He added a blanket and the teddy bear he bought when he got his new glasses. Then he picked up his nephew. Joey gurgled and rocked in his arms. "Mom thinks 'money' is a cross between Mommy and Nana." He made a face. "Money," he crooned.

"Money," Joey echoed.

"The money—" Matt began.

"*Money!*" Joey shouted it.

"If those plastic bags don't hold, it's going to stink." They'd put the money into thin plastic bags from the market produce section. Matt was beginning to wish that they'd sprung for the thicker freezer bags.

Lewis laid the baby in his crib. "Then we'll wash it."

Maybe that was what was meant by laundering money.

Nah.

Salty's fishing charters—tours.

Captain Henry Wardlow squinted up at his visitors from the deck of the *Salty 3*. He was stripped to the waist in the hot August sunlight. His bald head and the mat of gray hair on his chest glittered with perspiration. "What can I do for you two gents to-day? Interested in doing some fishing? Sightseeing?"

"Talk." Gerry jumped down on the deck. "We want to talk about a friend of ours."

Ed followed. "Our friend Charlie."

The captain looked about uneasily. "I don't think I know any Charlie."

"Charlie Swenson," Gerry said. "At the end of June you took him on a short tour up north. Remember? He died—"

"Oh, right. Say, I was really sorry to hear about that. I was taking him back to the city when he told me to take a detour here . . . something about wanting to look in on his daughter. When he didn't come back, I figured he'd decided to stay on." The man automatically backed away as Gerry came closer. "He said to wait for him, see? I waited all afternoon."

"He had a suitcase with him. We want it."

"He took the case with him," the man blustered. "It was brown, right? Like a briefcase? He scraped it as he got out, put a scratch clear across it."

"Hey, Hank!" A passing man called from the dock. "Oops, sorry, I guess you're working."

Ed moved his jacket to one side to give the older man a brief glimpse of his gun.

"Answer him," Gerry ordered in a low voice.

Hank moistened his lips. "Working. Right."

The man on the dock didn't move. "If you two

want to go out on a real craft, maybe you'd better come with me. This sieve can barely float." He laughed. "Just a joke."

Gerry had taken a small pocketknife from his pocket. He flicked it open. "Laugh," he ordered the sweating captain.

Hank barely showed his teeth. "Huh-huh-huh—" The sound resembled machinery that needed oiling.

The man laughed again and moved on.

Gerry began cleaning under his nails.

"Gents—" Hank was pale under his tan. "Now, look. We've worked for the same people. You know that. That's how Charlie knew about me." He forced a laugh. "I run errands, nothing too complicated. I ask no questions, nobody tells me anything."

Ed nudged him, and he stumbled against the bulkhead. "He doesn't ask questions."

"See," Gerry said, "the thing is that you were the last person to see Charlie with that suitcase."

"He left with it! I told you. I didn't even know what was in the suitcase. I didn't want to know."

"He doesn't know," Gerry said with an ugly laugh.

"Doesn't ask questions," Ed echoed.

"Maybe he was carrying underwear samples," the man said. "Vitamins. None of my business. He pays my way, I go where he wants. I wait, he doesn't come back."

"We will come back." Gerry turned away.

"Count on it," Ed said.

"When we do, we want you to tell us where our friend's suitcase is . . . for sentimental reasons." He gestured with the little knife. "Don't get any kind of idea of sailing away into the sunset. Some people would consider that an admission of guilt. We'll find you."

"But how am I—"

"Hey," Gerry snapped. "You don't tell me how to do my job. I don't tell you how to do yours."

"Another thing," Ed said.

The man's eyes were blank with fear. "What?"

"If I decide I want to do a little fishing while I'm here, how much would you charge me to take me out?"

Gerry shoved the man's shoulder. "That's assuming you find some information. Otherwise you get to be bait."

Ed snorted. "A lot you know about fishing. For bait, we'd have to cut him up."

"True," Gerry said as they left. "Very true."

MATT WANTED TO get a really great present for his dad's wedding. He saw himself giving his dad and Daisy keys to a new car, say. Or a boat. (After the reception, they were spending a couple of days on a friend's boat, then flying to Hawaii.)

No good. Then he remembered seeing something in Wong's storeroom and his heart jumped into his throat. Perfecto. When he told Lewis, his friend agreed.

In fact, Lewis offered to rig up a remote control. Sara Lee thought the idea was great. The only problem was that Wong's stock wasn't sufficient for what they planned.

Dermot agreed to drive across the border to buy them what they wanted. "Might as well," he grumbled. "There isn't enough room in my place to swing a cat. I'll buy gas while I'm down south." Gasoline in Potts was expensive, and the van had an extra tank. "It's time to make the last payment on my book, so I'll want the rest of my cash."

This was good. This was really good.

Matt's present wouldn't cost a whole lot, but it would make a big, big impression on everybody.

He'd give Jack and Daisy a wedding day they'd never forget.

"ASK HER IF SHE HAS A LUCKY PENNY FOR HER SHOE,"
Matt's grandmother said as she passed Jack.

Jack was sitting on the couch, talking on the phone
with Daisy. It was two o'clock on the afternoon of the
wedding, which was scheduled for five.

Mrs. Snow was fussing because Jack hadn't yet
changed out of his jeans and sweatshirt. In fact, he'd
just been out mowing the front lawn even though Matt
had been about to take care of it. Jack said he felt better
if he kept moving. His wedding suit hung in his room,
to be put on at the last minute.

Jack glanced up at his mother, then said something
into the phone. Daisy's question crackled over the
wires. Jack laughed. "Darned if I know."

"Here." Mrs. Snow reached for the phone. "Let
me speak to her." He hesitated. "You'll have the rest
of your lives."

Jack relinquished the phone. "More superstitions,
right?"

"Precautions." Mrs. Snow cradled the receiver

against her shoulder. "Good afternoon, Daisy. How is the bride?"

Superstitions. Matt had been hearing them for days. His grandmother was an expert on everything necessary to start a new marriage correctly, and she didn't mind sharing her knowledge. She had returned early from her vacation in Scotland armed to the teeth with wedding lore. She also brought Matt a thick cream-colored sweater that smelled like the sheep was still wearing it.

Happy is the bride the sun shines upon. Matt squinted out the window at a gloriously bright day.

Sunshine. Check.

Although the wedding would be at the church, the Come Back Café was catering the garden reception. For the past week, Jack had the regular staff working overtime to prepare food for the large number of expected guests. Matt had been helping as well.

Getting married took a lot of work. He mentioned that to his father the last time he came into the café kitchen to check on preparations.

"Trust me," Jack said, "the real work comes with being married. But the benefits are worth it."

Actually, Matt was enjoying himself. He liked the combination of food and everybody going crazy at once, swearing that nothing was going to be ready in time. Maybe he'd be a caterer when he grew up.

———————

"JACK, YOU SIMPLY may not see the bride before the wedding."

Apparently Daisy was having a bad case of nerves and Jack wanted to drive over to calm her.

"Mom, I've seen the bride. It's not like I just ordered her out of the Sears catalogue. I'm not planning to back out."

"It is bad luck—"

While they were arguing, Matt got on his bike and rode to the nearby house where Daisy rented a tiny basement apartment. He expected to find her alone. Instead, he found several other women, all wearing look-alike blue dresses.

Apparently superstition was contagious. The bridesmaid who answered the door stared at him. "I don't know whether the son of the groom is allowed to see the bride."

Daisy rushed out in jeans and a button-down denim shirt. Her hair looked sculpted, like a frozen whipped dessert. Her eyes were wide and panic-stricken. "Jack! Is Jack here?"

"Grandma won't let him," Matt said. "She keeps heading him off. How are you doing?"

"Awful. I'll probably trip going down the aisle."

"Which would you rather do?" Matt asked. "Get married or face a serial killer?"

One of the bridesmaids giggled. "He's sweet."

Sweet. Great.

"Excuse me." Jack's voice came from the doorway. "I understand that I'm needed in here."

General screeching. Before Matt's stunned eyes, the other women fanned out in front of Daisy like cows forming a circle around their young during a wolf attack.

Daisy's sister, who was her matron of honor, spoke up. "You're not allowed to come here."

Jack laughed. "It's okay. I'm invited to the wedding."

Daisy ducked around the others and hurled herself into his arms. Jack staggered slightly as he caught her. "Oh, Jack!" she wailed. "I couldn't go through this with anybody else."

He rested his chin against her forehead. "I hope not."

"You know what I mean." For a while they stood there like that. Like they were completely alone. Then Daisy seemed to realize that they weren't and that she was getting married in two hours. She backed up, blinking. "Thanks. I'm okay now. I don't know why I—"

"Bridal nerves," Matt said knowledgeably.

He didn't think he'd said anything particularly funny, but the bridesmaids all started laughing. It didn't take *anything* to set them off.

Daisy looked at her watch. "Oh, lord, I'd better

start getting dressed." She backed away and Jack slowly let her go. "See you later."

He grinned and headed toward the door. "See you."

Matt followed him out with a bunch of women repeating "cute" and "utterly adorable" behind his back.

Jack didn't sag until they stood before the car. "I wish you were old enough to drive." He held out his hands, palm-down. They looked steady enough to Matt. "I wish we'd decided on a morning wedding. That way everything would be over." He paused. "Could've caught the Jays game on TV this afternoon." He waited. "That's a joke, son."

If they had gotten married in the morning, that would have messed up the surprise that Matt and Lewis had planned.

Jack took out his keys. "I'll see you back at the house. Remember, the wedding's at five. You have to hand me the ring."

"Thanks, Dad." Like otherwise he'd forget.

He pedaled over to Lewis' house. "Is the remote ready?" he asked when his friend opened the door.

"No problem. I tested it out last night in the back-yard." He paused. "My dad helped me. He thinks it's a great idea."

Since Lewis had bought his new glasses, he and his father had almost seemed on good terms. That was good, because Mr. Rannulf had worked with detonation devices, and they needed all the help they could get with the wedding present.

"I CAN'T GET this stupid thing right." Matt stood before the hallway mirror, trying to make his tie cooperate.

"Let me see," his grandmother said. She began doing something swift and magical with his tie. "I often used to assist your grandfather. There." She adjusted the lapels of his jacket. "You look very handsome. Sometimes I see your mother in you." Her jaw gave a convulsive twitch that was over so quickly Matt almost thought he had imagined it.

"You're looking good, too," he said awkwardly.

She was all dressed up in a violet suit. Her eyelids were violet as well, whereas Daisy had stuff on her eyelids that made them look shiny and multicolored, like guppies.

His grandmother examined herself in the mirror. She patted her hair, which looked like she'd had it styled at the same place as Daisy. "Not bad, if I do say so myself."

THEN IT WAS over and everybody was kissing everybody else. Matt didn't drop the ring as he feared, and Daisy didn't start giggling or trip as she feared, and Jack's hands seemed steady. ("Cold," Daisy confided to Matt later. "Ice cold. I was definitely beginning to reconsider.")

"You have lipstick next to your ear," Lewis said.

Matt was standing near his dad and new step-mother, receiving congratulations. He reached up to touch his right ear.

"Other ear. Both ears, actually. Chin, too."

The way Lewis was describing it, Matt felt he must look like an Indian in an old western. "I got nailed by a couple of bridesmaids."

"Yeah, I saw. You didn't seem to be fighting back."

He wasn't really complaining. The prettiest one got him on the lips, then said she wanted to dance with him later. He figured she was seventeen.

Matt shrugged. "What can I say?"

Lewis wasn't wearing a suit because he didn't own one, and of course he couldn't exactly buy one with the cash. He did get new slacks and a purple shirt, and he had his black shoes from band. His mother had borrowed a jacket that reeked of cigarette smoke but fit okay. She'd even stuck a folded handkerchief in his breast pocket.

Dermot was scheduled to meet them later at the reception, after everyone had eaten. The surprise was in his van. He'd also promised to help set things up and get everything started so Matt and Lewis could stay with the main crowd.

"HE'S NOT HERE," Matt said worriedly to Lewis. "They're already cutting the cake." He checked his watch for what had to be the millionth time. Almost seven-thirty. Dermot was supposed to arrive by seven.

"Maybe he fell asleep."

"You don't think he's . . ." He didn't finish the sentence. He didn't have to.

Drunk.

Lewis groaned. "He wouldn't do that, not today."

"He might."

Matt cast a worried glance at the bridal couple. It seemed like everybody had brought a camera to take photographs of Jack and Daisy feeding each other bits of cake from their fingers.

Because the café employees were invited to the wedding and reception, Jack had hired help from outside to serve the food and drinks. Matt had suggested Sara Lee, who had done some waitressing. So she was there, too, dressed in black slacks and a white blouse, with her hair tied back.

She stopped next to him when she was walking around with a coffeepot. "You're looking pretty good tonight. I like your stepmother. She's funny."

Sara was the only other person who knew the details of the surprise.

Matt looked at his watch again. "Dermot's not here yet and a couple of people have already left." Those were people with little kids at home and baby-sitters, but he was still worried.

Sara frowned. "Maybe he forgot it was tonight."

"Crap." Matt looked around. "We'd better check on him." He waved for Lewis to come over. "Tell my dad that I'll be right back, okay?"

A portly woman was holding up her cup for a refill. Sara moved away. "Okay. I'll pass on the message."

Lewis' bicycle was in the garage with Matt's. "What do we do if Dermot's drunk?" he asked worriedly. There was too much for them to carry, and a taxi driver would never find Dermot's place in time.

Matt flexed his fingers. "I can drive the van. It's only a couple of miles." His father had given him informal driving lessons in the pickup. He'd run the van a couple of times, too, although never off the side road leading to Dermot's property.

"Great. And if you get caught—"

"Who's going to catch me?"

Lewis looked back at the wedding crowd. "Good point."

Daisy's replacement officer was on duty that night in Potts. Daisy had just gotten married, and her sergeant had given away the bride. Right now he was eating cake, standing next to the table where she was beginning to unwrap her presents.

"I DON'T LIKE this," Lewis said as they wheeled their bikes down the dark road toward Dermot's cottage. "I do not, repeat, *not,* like this."

The van was parked near the cairn marking Dermot's property, meaning he was probably home. They had passed a parked tan sedan a short distance away.

As they rested their bikes against a tree, Matt could see a light shining inside the cottage below. "I think he has company," he said as shadows passed before the window.

"Great," Lewis said. "We get two old drunks for the price of one."

They froze at the sound of a harsh grunt. Something fell inside the cottage. "Falling down drunks," Lewis said with a grimace. "That's the best kind. No, the best kind is falling down drunks who get sick on your shoes."

Another crash.

"Maybe they're fighting," Matt whispered.

They walked toward the house quietly as the moon began rising above the ocean.

For a while there was silence, then a voice raised in anger. "Wouldn't I tell you by now?" That was Dermot. "I found it by the side of the road."

Matt knocked on the door. "Dermot? Are you okay?"

He heard a hurried consultation inside.

The door opened. Matt couldn't see the other man in the cottage. He and Lewis both stared at Dermot. The old man's face was bruised, and one eye was almost swollen shut.

"Jeez!" Matt gasped. "What happened to you?"

Dermot gave him a horrible mockery of a smile. "Been on a toot, my friend. I don't want to buy no candy bars today, so you two better run along." He looked around at the man who stood in the shadows. "These are kids from the local church."

Matt supposed he and Lewis were dressed like they had come from church. In a sense, they had. Was Dermot so drunk that he couldn't recognize them?

He smelled sour, all right, like he'd been swimming in booze. His shirt was stained and the buttons torn so that more bruises showed on his scrawny chest. Another smell rose off him to mix with the others, stronger than the rest although Matt couldn't recognize it straight off.

They had a reception to go back to, a surprise to be set up, and Dermot had gotten juiced. "What about my stuff?" Matt demanded.

"I told you," Dermot said in an ugly voice. "I don't want to buy your candy." He started to shut the door. "Go on. Scram."

A wood stove stood open against the opposite wall. Inside, Matt saw the red covers of Dermot's notebook. Pages had been torn out and burned so that only their corners remained. That's all he saw before the door to the shack closed firmly.

Lewis had seen it, too. "He'd never burn his poems," he whispered as they started back toward their bikes.

Matt stopped. "Something's really wrong."

They sneaked down to listen under the window, trying not to make any noise in the loose gravel.

"I told you a thousand times," Dermot was protesting. "I found that damned suitcase by the side of the road. It looked like it still had some wear, so I brought it home."

The suitcase! Matt sucked in his breath. He had used it as a container for his CDs.

"Sure. And tell me again about the electronics in the boxes. You won a lottery, right? Only you can't remember which lottery."

"Okay, okay." Dermot's laugh sounded forced. "So I'm a small businessman. You boys understand that. Maybe I don't have receipts for everything. Let's say it fell off a boat."

Now Dermot was claiming he had stolen the stuff he'd bought for them.

The man spoke. "Let's say that I didn't exactly fall off the cabbage truck myself. You have receipts. I saw them. Let's talk about the suitcase again."

Matt and Lewis rose up slightly, but their view was blocked by the man's back.

"We have to get help," Lewis whispered. "Dermot's getting hurt."

"I wouldn't do that," a deep voice said behind them.

They turned slowly. Looked up. Way up. "Hi," Matt said.

He must have come from the outhouse.

Lewis' voice squeaked as he spoke. "We belong to a church youth group. Maybe you'd like to buy our candy."

Hands like giant steel clamps closed on their shoulders. "I don't eat candy."

"That's good," Lewis babbled. "That way you don't get cavities."

"Shut up," Matt hissed. The next thing he knew, Lewis would be offering to sell him tofu. He recognized the odor emanating from Dermot, because now it was coming off of him.

It was fear.

"Hey, Gerry!" The man's voice rose. "You have company. Kids." They were led into the shack. "I found these two sneaking around outside. This one—" He shook Lewis like a puppy. "He said they were selling candy."

"There's the kind with nuts," Matt said desperately. "And then there's pure milk chocolate. I know that five dollars a bar sounds like a lot, but it's for a real good cause." He tried to smile. He didn't know what he'd do if they actually wanted to buy a candy bar.

The slighter man pointed to his head. "I'm beginning to put two and one together." Receipts lay on the table for everything they'd been buying. He walked over and began leafing through them, reading the names at the top. "Which of you is Matthew Snow?"

"I told you," Dermot protested. "I stole everything."

Without even looking at him, the man backhanded him across the face. Dermot staggered. He came up spitting blood.

Tears stung Matt's eyes. "Me," he managed. "I'm Matt Snow."

"And you're Lewis Rannulf."

Lewis gulped and nodded.

The big man let them go, but he didn't move away. Matt looked around wildly for a way to escape. Too many boxes separated them from the windows.

Both men had guns. He saw that now.

"Well, boys," Gerry said. "I think you have something that doesn't belong to you."

"Money," Ed intoned.

CHAPTER
17

"I WONDER WHERE THE BOYS HAVE GONE," DAISY RE-marked to her new husband.

Jack looked around. "They said something about a surprise."

"Oh, good." Daisy laughed. "I love surprises."

As Jack hugged his bride, her wedding dress rustled against him. "Where there are kids, you can count on plenty of those."

"Then I'll have something to look forward to. I just hope that they didn't spend too much on our wedding present. They've been working so hard this summer."

"They're good kids." He released her slowly. "Sara said they had to go out for a while. But that was some time ago." Jack squinted out toward the growing darkness. "I wonder where they are."

LEWIS WAS TRYING to stop the bleeding on Dermot's forehead with the handkerchief from his pocket. "It's all right, boy," the old man said as he took it from him. "It just looks bad."

"We're supposed to be at a wedding," Matt said,

trying to keep his voice steady. "People will miss us."

"Are you getting married?" Gerry asked. "Unless one of you is the groom, trust me, you won't be missed."

"It's my dad's wedding." Matt could have added that his father was marrying a Mountie. He didn't because then their captors would know that Potts had even fewer police on duty than usual.

"If your father's getting married—" Gerry spoke easily—"I guess you'll want to get back as soon as possible. See, if you don't get back at all, you might spoil his honeymoon."

That was when Matt and Lewis both started talking at once, tripping over their words. The money was at Lewis' house. No problem. The two men could have it. They hadn't spent much.

"A crib mattress." Gerry started to laugh, which seemed a good sign.

"My folks are at a movie tonight," Lewis said. "My sister went to visit some friends. Nobody's home."

Gerry's smile smoothed out. "I hope not."

THE TWO MEN talked together, then decided that everybody would have to go. Although they could all fit in the tan sedan, it would be a tight squeeze. Besides, like Ed said, after the money was handed over, they would go their separate ways.

The way they arranged it was that Dermot drove

the van while Gerry sat in the passenger seat and Matt and Lewis occupied the backseat. Ed followed behind in the tan sedan.

Matt's wedding gift lay on the floor under the seat in several wrapped bundles. "I think we can arrange for you to keep the merchandise you bought," Gerry said smoothly, "if you cooperate. Call it a finder's fee."

Gerry was holding a gun. He didn't have to give them anything. Matt's throat felt so choked that he could hardly breathe. Next to him, Lewis sniffed. Scared. Matt had never been so scared in his life. The side of his arm touched Lewis' arm. Lewis was trembling. They both were.

Neither boy said anything.

THE TWO BOYS went inside Lewis' house accompanied by Gerry. "I don't want anybody to get cute," the man warned.

Matt had never felt less cute in his entire life, despite what the bridesmaids had said.

They headed straight for Lewis' room. The baby's crib was made up with the teddy bear sitting inside. Lewis began stripping off the sheet. He stopped, gaping like he couldn't believe his eyes, then tore off the rest of the bedding. The sheet and blue blanket dropped from his fingers onto the floor.

When he turned toward them, Lewis' face was

white. "This isn't it." His voice was high and strained. "This isn't the same crib mattress. The other one was all taped up. This is a different one. Newer."

Gerry scowled. "I told you not to get cute."

This one was blue, too, but not the turquoise shade that Matt remembered. "It's not the same mattress."

He and Lewis stared at each other.

"Wait." Lewis shoved past them toward the living room. "Corinne left a number."

"Corinne's his sister," Matt explained. "It's her baby."

In the living room, Lewis looked around wildly. "It's here somewhere. There." He reached down for a slip of paper, bumping his head on the coffee table, then straightened. He reached for the phone.

Gerry blocked him with the hand that held the gun. "No telephone."

Lewis held up the paper. "This is where my sister is tonight. I'll call her. She'll know."

"No phone."

"It's not the right mattress." He barely whispered.

Matt's mind whirled. "Didn't your mother buy baby stuff at a garage sale last weekend? You said you were crowded out."

"I have to call Corinne," Lewis repeated. "Don't you want your money? Sure to God you don't want to wait . . ."

Lewis didn't finish. His eyes seemed magnified behind his glasses, almost black. If the gunmen waited long enough, his family would come home.

His dad.

His mom.

Corinne.

Joey was only nine months old.

"If my dad starts looking for me," Matt said, "this is the first place he'll come."

"Okay," Gerry said at last. "Dial. Give the receiver to me." He transferred the gun to his other hand. They all held their breath as the phone rang. Once. twice. The third ring didn't finish. Gerry handed the receiver to Lewis. "Talk."

Matt could hear tinny music in the background. "Is Corinne there? It's Lewis." He waited. "I'm at the house. The wedding was okay. Corinne, what happened to the old crib mattress?" Matt could hear her laughing. Lewis' face fell. He looked sick. "All right. See you later. Corinne, take care of Joey, okay?"

"So where's the mattress?" Gerry asked as he hung up.

Lewis cleared his throat. "They put it out for the trash collector three days ago. It's at the dump."

To the dump, to the dump, to the dump-dump-dump. He and Lewis used to set it to music.

By now, Matt thought glumly as they drove up the

winding road between Potts and Upper Potts, the people at the wedding absolutely had to realize he was missing. No matter how good a time everybody was having, they must wonder where he was.

Not that anybody would think of looking for him at the Potts Town Dump.

At least it wasn't far. Ed and Gerry took the turnoff onto a narrow gravel road with a ditch on either side. Lewis had already explained that Potts didn't have a huge dump like the city. It was the size of a hockey rink. Chances were that they could spot the mattress just by walking around. It was blue. Turquoise. Thick. Mended with tape.

"It looks like we walk from here," Gerry announced when they reached a wire chain. Someone had dumped a small trailer load of trash outside the chain. The bulk of Potts' garbage was directly inside in heaps of varying sizes.

They got out. Even though the trip had been short, Matt's muscles were cramped.

He could see one big problem already. There were only two tall lamp poles in the dumping ground, one at each side, plus a third outside the chain in the parking area. The light was so faint that it barely illuminated the ground. Their faces seemed a sick yellow. All around him were a jumble of angles and hooks and cubes of all sizes.

Dermot had already told them that he carried no

flashlights. Ed searched the car anyway, while Gerry kept a gun on them. He called out the items in the back. "Painting supplies . . . bag of fertilizer . . . newspapers . . . empty bottles." He looked under the backseat. "What's this?"

"They're for the wedding reception," Matt answered.

He unwrapped the first bundle, looked inside, glanced at the boys, then replaced it. Grunting, he got out of the van, leaving the side door open wide.

"Okay," Gerry announced, "this is the buddy system, like at camp. Everybody is responsible for a buddy. That means that if anybody decides to stroll away, he shouldn't expect to see his buddies alive again. Got it?"

They got it.

So THERE WAS Matt in his wedding suit and new shoes, slipping around in garbage that oozed and stank, while broken glass splintered under his feet. Next to him was Lewis in his new clothes. Dermot kept staggering around and apologizing. He'd been drinking, he said. He talked too much at a local tavern. Somebody must have overheard him.

The two guys stayed with them, making sure that nobody tried to get away. Making sure they didn't dash for freedom through the trees and prickle bushes.

"They put the crib mattress out with the regular

trash," Lewis said when Matt started to turn over a full-sized mattress to see if anything was underneath. "Don't waste time on big stuff like this. The sanitation workers only take small things."

The truck in Potts wasn't exactly huge. Matt was surprised they had picked up the mattress at all.

They both walked along. "Do you think they're going to kill us?" Matt asked Lewis softly.

"They might." That didn't make him feel any better. "I don't think they want witnesses. Maybe that's why they wanted to take the van. If I wanted to kill us, I'd make it look like Dermot drove off a cliff. Two kids dead. Too bad."

Matt choked back a sob and tried to concentrate on finding the mattress. Lewis was wrong. He had to be. "But they were talking about letting us keep the stuff we bought."

"Yeah. Well, they would, wouldn't they?"

"Don't talk," Gerry snapped. "Just keep looking."

Matt could see shapes of things, but colors were hard to distinguish in the eerie light. "Sorry," he whispered to Lewis when they bent over to move some bags. "Sorry I suggested the beach trail that day."

"Sorry I slipped on the beach trail."

Matt was sorry they'd ever found the money, sorry they hadn't turned it in.

Really sorry they had gotten caught.

"JACK, YOU NEVER mentioned that you took Matt to Disneyland," Mrs. Snow said. She was sipping from a glass of fruit punch which contained something extra that was quite nice.

Next to her, her new daughter-in-law looked as though she wished she could remove her evening slippers. A nice girl, really. Mrs. Snow was prepared to report back to her friends that Daisy didn't seem at all like a police officer.

"I haven't gotten around to taking him on any kind of vacation in a long time." Jack drank down his own punch. "He's dropped enough hints about southern California."

"But the photographs," Mrs. Snow protested. "I'm sure that was Disneyland. Matt and Lewis were standing in front of Sleeping Beauty's castle, and there was a man with them." They were both staring at her as though she was insane. "I found an envelope of pictures in Matt's sweater drawer. I'll get them."

A few minutes later she was back. "They were developed a few weeks ago."

Wordlessly Jack took the pictures. While Daisy looked on, he moved aside a gift espresso maker and spread the photographs on the table.

"I don't understand," he said. "When could they have gone?"

"You mean you don't know?" his mother asked.

Jack picked up one photograph. "That's Dermot with them."

Daisy's laugh was shaky. "Is this one of those surprises you were telling me about?"

"Matt!" Jack looked around. "I don't know what is going on, but I want an explanation *now*." He waited. *"Matt!"* he bellowed. "Lewis!"

Daisy tugged at his sleeve. "Remember, they went out."

"Then where the hell are they?"

"Oh, dear," Mrs. Snow said faintly. "I do hope that everything is all right."

"Everything is *not* all right."

Daisy's lips tightened as she picked up another photo showing three faces, two smiling and one grim. "Obviously something has been happening. But let's wait until we speak with the boys."

Jack went inside to phone Lewis' house.

AS THEY WALKED past the rubble, kicking at suspicious-looking mounds and occasionally leaning to inspect their findings, both boys avoided looking at the huge incinerator at the back of the dump where garbage was burned. Matt thought burning had been halted because the summer was so dry, but the possibility existed that the mattress and its contents had been ash for three days.

So far, they had found every disgusting piece of trash in Potts, some of which they couldn't identify because the light was so poor.

"I located some kind of mattress," Dermot called abruptly. "Come see if it's yours."

Matt and Lewis hurried over, followed closely by Gerry. As they reached Dermot, Matt slipped and grabbed at a handle sticking out of a pile of trash. He ended up sitting on his rear with a rusty pogo stick in his hand.

"You don't have time to play," Gerry said, gesturing with his gun.

Matt threw the pogo stick away. It landed nearby with a splat. When he went to wipe his hands on his jacket, he was puzzled for a minute because he was carrying something in his pocket that was the size of a deck of cards.

Then he remembered what it was.

Lewis was dragging out the mattress Dermot found. He stopped.

"Is that the right one?" Gerry asked.

Lewis shook his head. "This is from a youth bed."

Ed nudged it with his foot. "What's a youth bed?"

"A youth bed is for kids too big for a crib but not ready for a regular bed." Lewis straightened. "This one is blue, all right, but it's too big."

"I saw the crib," Gerry said finally. "The kid's right."

"Crap." Ed looked around. "This place isn't exactly a perfume factory." He glowered at Lewis. "How about if you stop wasting time? Then we can all get out of here."

"I want to go home," Matt said loudly. He dug into the heap again, but this time as though it were his dessert. "I want to find that mattress." He hurled aside two more garbage bags, followed that with two more. "After this, I don't care if I never see that money again."

Lewis stood there watching him with his mouth open.

"This isn't rest period," Gerry told him.

"You're the one who found the suitcase in the first place," Matt yelled at Lewis. "How come you're just standing there? Give me a hand pulling this out." *This* looked like part of somebody's barbecue, but that was all right. He was waiting until Lewis leaned close, then he planned to whisper that he had the remote control that would set off the wedding present.

As they pulled out an old fender, a crib mattress fell almost on top of them.

"There!" Dermot yelled triumphantly. "That's a damned blue crib mattress, and nobody can say that it's not."

They all stared at it. "Is this the one?" Gerry asked.

The mattress was thick. It had a lot of mending tape like the one with the money.

"I don't know." Lewis didn't sound like he was lying.

"You don't know," Gerry echoed.

"It's this light," Lewis said. "It makes it hard to see. Hey, I didn't exactly memorize what the mattress looked like. I never even took the sheet off all the way. I didn't think it was going anywhere. I never thought—"

He never thought his life would depend on it.

"Rip off some of that tape," Gerry said.

Although Gerry could have been talking to any of them, Ed knelt down. He began to rip off a strip of tape. "Back up. I can't see anything." He ripped off more tape. He was about to put his fingers inside when he halted at the sound of a siren wailing somewhere below.

It was the ambulance going somewhere in a hurry, although Matt didn't think the men would know that. "The police are probably looking for us," he said desperately. "Maybe you could take the mattress and get out of here, and then we could all go and we wouldn't say anything to anybody. Honest to God."

Lewis gulped. "That's the mattress. I'm sure of it."

The sound of the siren faded away.

The two men consulted quickly. Ed was saying something about not wanting to put his hand inside if he didn't have better light. Rats could be nesting inside. Snakes.

"You kids," Gerry instructed them. "Carry the mattress back to the van."

Yes!

"Let the boys go," Dermot pleaded as each boy grabbed an end of the mattress. It was heavier than it looked, probably from the amount of slime it had absorbed sitting in a puddle at the dump. "You have what you came for. None of us can afford to say anything. Nobody has clean hands."

Matt almost laughed at that because his hands and the rest of him were filthy. He didn't. He had the feeling that if he started laughing, he wouldn't be able to stop.

Closer. They were getting closer to the van. The shapes were beginning to look familiar, almost like old friends.

The only problem was that his arms were full of mattress. He needed both hands free. He also needed not to be watched for a minute.

In the faint yellow light he saw the loosely wrapped bundles inside the van, under the seat. He touched the control in his pocket for reassurance.

"I gotta pee," Matt announced suddenly.

"Wait until the mattress is in the car," Gerry said. "We're almost there."

Matt started dancing around, which made Lewis slip with his end of the mattress. "No kidding, I have to go. It's a medical thing. My school knows about it and everything."

Lewis was looking at him with a puzzled expression.

"Here," Ed said, taking Matt's end of the mattress. "Lean this thing next to the van."

"Where do you think you're going?" Gerry asked.

"Just over here," Matt said, stopping at a pile of trash that stood a short distance from the open door. He turned away, all too aware that he was being watched.

"I think it's the right mattress," Lewis said.

"Gerry, give me your knife," Ed said. "I'll lay this thing open."

Matt was looking at the control, which Lewis' dad had converted from the remote for a toy tank. Lewis had showed him how to use it, but he'd never tried it out.

Gerry was looking through his pockets. "For somebody who really had to go, this kid is taking long enough to water the daisies."

"He's probably not used to going tinkle in a dump."

Matt turned slowly. "I don't think I can go after all. Is that the money?" The two men glanced down at the mattress. Matt pointed the control toward the open door and pressed what he hoped was the FIRE button.

Please, he prayed. Please, please, please.

NOTHING HAPPENED.

At first.

Ed sniffed. "Do you smell something burning?"

"This is a dump," Gerry said in disgust. "I can smell my worst nightmare. Go on, open that mattress." He turned slightly. "You three, stay together."

Ed ripped off some more tape. He started to reach inside the mattress but stopped. "No kidding, I smell smoke." He looked into the van.

"Maybe I left my pipe," Dermot offered.

"That's no tobacco."

Matt could hear it now, a faint hissing coming from the brown paper-wrapped bundle on the floor. He tried to glance casually toward it. A tiny tongue of flame licked out, neatly folding back the paper.

"Hey!" he yelled, pointing at a nearby pile. "I see another crib mattress over there."

"Where?" Gerry craned his neck.

"I haven't checked this one out yet," Ed complained.

Sssssssssssssssssssssssssssssssssssssssssssssssssssssss. The first Roman candle took off, screaming between the two men as it headed toward the nearest garbage heap, exploding in a shower of red and silver sparks.

"What the—" Gerry yelled.

Matt's wedding present to his father and Daisy began exploding inside the van. It was fireworks. And the remote had set them off.

Ssssssssssssssssssssssssssssssssssssssssssssssssssss.

Ssssssssssssssssssssssssssssssssssssssssssssssssssss.

Two more Roman candles went off. The blue and silver one traveled farther this time. None of them went up, which was what would have to happen if they were to be seen from the main road.

A flare, that's what Matt had wanted.

Something to tell his dad where he was.

Ssssssssssssssssssssssssssssssssssssssssssssssssssss.

Another Roman candle lit up the van with golden sparks. The two men stood there gaping.

"Come on!" Lewis started running toward the nearest bushes.

Matt thought that Dermot was running as well, but he lost sight of him as they headed through a thicket of blackberry vines. There was loud *bang* from the direction of the van and a hot stabbing in his arm. All Matt could think was that a thorn had gotten him, tearing his jacket. A thorn, sure. He stumbled and Lewis smashed into him. "We have to get farther away from the light," Lewis gasped, running onward. "Find somewhere really thick—fast. Then don't move."

Multicolored sparks and explosions were still coming from the direction of the van. They were in the
darkness surrounded by thorns, followed by men with
guns. Matt held up one arm to keep his face from being
scratched up. The thorn that had gotten his other arm
had really been lethal. Blood was trickling down.

Lewis pulled at that arm and Matt gasped.

"In here," Lewis directed.

Matt half fell against a rock, then he and Lewis crept
into a space between two bushes. He couldn't hear
anybody moving outside, but that didn't mean they
weren't there. "The fireworks went off sideways," he
whispered. "Nobody's going to see them."

"Sh-h-h."

Somebody was stumbling around in the dark,
swearing.

Gerry.

"Did you find them?" Ed called from a short distance away.

"Not yet."

Matt tried to shrink.

"Anyway, the old man's not going anywhere."

Lewis' glasses were shining in the moonlight. Matt
gestured, and he shaded them with his hand. "Maybe
it's a trick," he whispered as Ed moved on.

"Maybe."

"Come on," Gerry said after another minute.
"Let's take the mattress and get out of here."

Neither man moved.

That was definitely a trick.

"It sounds like the fireworks are about done," Ed said.

Gerry turned back to the road. He stopped. "Look what I see. Two kids." He was looking totally in the opposite direction. Matt relaxed. He didn't really see them.

Only, Dermot didn't know that. Suddenly he yelled out from the other side of the chain. "I'm over here, you bastards! Come and get me!"

Both boys raised their heads slightly. From inside the prickle bushes Matt could see Dermot walking out from behind the van, calmly lighting his pipe. Dermot was holding something else, too. A bottle.

"Come on down," he called. "Have a friendly drink."

The bottle didn't look right. In the dim light it looked like a rag was coming out of it. Dermot lit another match. He held it up. "All right, I want to see the boys now. And I want to see them safe."

"It's a Molotov cocktail!" Ed yelled.

Gerry took quick aim and fired. Dermot staggered.

Before the man could fire again, Matt leaped out of the bush and tackled him, forgetting about his sore arm. Maybe the man didn't go down, but he managed to make him drop the gun. Then something smashed into his skull.

LEWIS AND ED both ran for the van. The man was bigger and faster. He also fell harder when his foot tangled in some vines.

Lewis kept on running.

Dermot was still holding the bottle, trying to light another match. His shirt was dark-stained near the shoulder. "Get out of here!" he snarled at the boy. "They know what I can do with this thing. I can hold them off for a few minutes."

"They'll kill you." The rag was Lewis' handkerchief.

The match flared. "*Run,* damn your hide!" Dermot shouted as the handkerchief caught fire.

Ed was stumbling toward them. He stopped uncertainly, his face pasty under the yellow light as he raised his gun.

Gerry was farther away. "Shoot him!"

Dermot held the bottle over the mattress as the flames began licking upward. "Go on," he tempted softly. "Shoot me."

The big man tensed. The gun began to shift toward Lewis. "I'll shoot him instead."

Like Lewis was just going to stand there.

Probably neither man expected him to do anything. Lewis grabbed the bottle from Dermot's hand and hurled it inside the van, toward the back. Toward the sacks of fertilizer and the alcohol and paint solvents.

"Get down!" Dermot yelled.

Lewis tried to dive toward the pile of trash, but something shoved him the other way and he fell.

THAT WAS WHEN the van exploded.

Then the sedan.

MATT LAY ON the ground, feeling like he'd been kicked in the head. Maybe he had.

Looking straight up into the nighttime sky, he saw fireworks.

CHAPTER
19

"WAS THAT A SONIC BOOM?" MRS. SNOW ASKED HER new daughter-in-law as they stood in the garden. The windows of the house were vibrating from the force of an explosion somewhere in the nearby hills.

A second blast followed immediately, only slightly less emphatic than the first.

Daisy looked puzzled. "It's late in the day for blasting." Jack had gone to Lewis' house to find the boys. "I think I'll phone Lewis' house to see whether . . ."

Frustratingly, Daisy left the sentence unfinished as she headed into the house. Mrs. Snow followed.

The telephone was ringing as they came into the living room. Daisy answered it. She listened for a moment, then covered the receiver. "Ron, please fetch the sergeant to the telephone. He's in back. Hurry." She went back on the phone. "Fred, if you can come around, we're saving you a slice of—" She stopped. "What?" She stood there. "Fireworks?"

Mrs. Snow noticed the pretty Chinese girl coming around with a tray. Daisy shook her head distractedly as Sara approached, and the girl moved on.

The sergeant came in from the garden.

"Something's going on at the dump," Daisy told him. "Explosions and now fireworks. Roman candles. Fred says it sounds like a regular show out there."

Mrs. Snow was about to take a small iced cake from Sara's tray. As she reached toward it, the tray was abruptly jerked away.

"Fireworks? Oh, my gosh!" Sara gasped. "Matt!"

IN FRONT OF the remains of the van, two men were yelling at each other, dancing around like members of a primitive tribe.

Matt didn't know what Lewis had done, but the explosion had taken out the overhead light in the parking area. The main part of the dump was still illuminated in sickly yellow, distorted by oily smoke from the blast.

After getting unsteadily to his feet, he took off, running straight past the piles of rubble, counting on the smoke to hide him. He jumped the chain, staggering when he came down. A Screaming Mimi went off, white sparks blossoming overhead as it shrieked. For a few seconds, everything was almost as light as day. If they were looking in his direction, they could see him.

Then it was dark again. He kept running, even though the pain in his arm had become a steady rush of fire. He couldn't stop. Their only chance was for him to reach the highway and find help.

"THE KID!" GERRY shouted. "Catch the kid!"

Ed took off after the taller of the two boys. The kid had come out of nowhere and had a good head start down the road. At least Gerry had found his gun again. He stayed behind to look for the smaller boy. Gerry wasn't a runner.

Ed was.

LEWIS MOANED. HE lay on top of what felt like slimy cardboard and bags of garbage. He was down in a ditch while the world burned above. Beyond that, stars glittered indifferently.

His new glasses were awry, and he moved automatically to straighten them. One lens dropped out. He held them away from his face. The other lens fell, going *plink* on a rock near his feet. He slid his fingers along the frame. One earpiece was bent at a weird angle.

Dermot! He didn't know what happened to him during the explosion.

Lewis struggled to his feet, dropping the twisted wire.

His ears were ringing as he caught a protruding rock and began to climb out of the chest-high ditch.

In the distance, he heard the wailing siren that called the Potts volunteer firemen from their homes. "Dermot—"

Illuminated in orange light from the still-blazing cars, the old man lay facedown nearby. "Dermot, are you okay?"

Nothing.

He smelled burning meat and gagged.

Loose gravel shifted under his feet, and he slid so that he had to flatten himself against the side of the ditch before he could start up again. "Dermot?" The form on the ground lay still. "Aw, Dermot."

A movement nearby made him freeze.

"There you are, you little creep."

He looked up slowly to see a man moving to the edge of the ditch. Looked up farther.

Gerry stood there, breathing hard. He had a gun in his hand. Swearing, he raised it toward Lewis.

At that moment, Lewis' mind went blank.

Vacant.

There was a slight movement beyond the ditch. Gerry stumbled as though something had struck him behind the knees.

Lewis let go of the side of the ditch with one hand and grabbed the man's ankle.

The gun clattered down as both fell into the dark ditch in a tangle of limbs. As a fist glanced off his shoulder, Lewis dived for the area where he thought the gun had landed. More blows landed on his back. He scarcely felt them.

He came up clutching a gun pointed at his own midsection. He managed to rotate it and was just turning when his legs were kicked out from under him.

Lewis landed on his back. Breathless, he pointed the gun upward. All he could see was Gerry's silhouette looming above him, a large rock in one upraised hand.

ED HAD LOST sight of the boy on the dark road, but he could still hear his shoes pounding ahead through the gravel. Then the boy entered the circle of light that marked the turnoff to the highway. He glanced behind him.

Bad move. The boy faltered.

"Give it up!" Ed yelled as he began to close the gap between them. "There's nothing around here but trees."

A small car was coming up the highway from the direction of the mill. Abruptly it swung onto the road, narrowly missing the boy. Passing him. It stopped directly in front of Ed, holding him captive in the glare of its headlights. He automatically threw his hands before his eyes.

The car door opened. A woman came partway out, and he found himself staring into the barrel of a police revolver. She crouched, resting her arms on the top of the door. "Hold it right there," she ordered. She was wearing a frothy white dress, evening slippers, and—unbelievably—a lace veil. "Put your hands on your head."

Slowly, he raised his hands.

The boy had come back. "My stepmother is a cop," he yelled. "If you make a move, she'll blow your head off."

Ed thought the bride winced.

"Are you all right, Matt?" she asked.

The boy nodded. "I'm okay. But Lewis and Dermot are still back there with the other guy."

LEWIS HAD NEVER held a gun before. "Bang!" he yelled at the shadowed form. He steadied the gun with his other hand like he'd seen on TV. At this range, he couldn't miss.

The man halted, dropping the rock. "Take it easy." He backed off, stumbling over the garbage in the ditch. "Careful. That thing might go off."

"You killed Dermot. Matt—" Lewis choked. "Bang!"

The man sucked in his breath. "Don't—"

Acrid smoke floated from the direction of the burning cars, stinging his eyes.

That's the way the money goes.
POP goes the weasel.

"Pop!" His finger tightened on the trigger.

Pebbles skittered lazily down the side. "Steady, Lewis," Dermot said in a soft voice. "Matt is all right. Don't shoot unless you have to. Help is coming up the road."

He had to concentrate on not shooting or it wasn't going to not happen. He waited, anticipating. All the man had to do was move one muscle.

"Kid—"

Lewis felt breathless, like he was about to open a birthday present. The fireworks had stopped, but multicolored sparks still danced in his head.

Dermot began talking again, his voice low and soothing.

About Disneyland.

The tram ride at Universal Studios.

The roller coasters.

About how he felt proud when they called him their grandfather.

Lewis breathed long and deep through his mouth. His hands were trembling. The ditch seemed to be getting darker.

At last he heard voices coming near.

"Over here," Dermot shouted. "Hurry!"

"It's all right, son," a man said a moment later. "Just relax."

Lewis stood there until the gun was taken from his hands. Even then, he had trouble releasing it. He took one last glance toward Gerry before he allowed himself to be helped out of the ditch by another policeman.

"You're dead," he said.

THEN THERE WERE lots of sirens.

The ambulance.

Fire trucks.

MATT COULD HARDLY believe it, but he was still alive. They were all alive.

Two of the most astonished gangsters he had ever seen—okay, he hadn't met any others—stood in the parking lot of the Potts dump surrounded by at least thirty police officers.

"A cop wedding?" Gerry yelled before he was led away. "This was a cop wedding?"

Cops and cooks.

Jack was among the last to arrive. By then, the area was so crowded with fire trucks and other official vehicles that he had to park at the side of the highway and walk up.

Matt was about to move toward his father except that the ground began to look crooked. He decided to sit down on the bumper of one of the cars instead. Then Jack was standing before him. "Hi, Dad," he said. "Sorry about the suit."

"Matt—" Jack stared at his arm. "You're hurt."

"Shot. I'm shot." Blood was dripping off his

fingers again. No big deal. That meant he was alive. "It's okay." He thought of something. "I don't have a wedding present for you anymore. The fireworks sort of went off." His father looked stunned. "You should've seen them. No kidding."

Nearby, ambulance attendants examined Dermot while the old man complained loudly. Lewis sat on the ground a short distance away with his head between his knees.

Sick, probably. Matt figured that Lewis had taken shelter after the explosion. He had missed the rest of the excitement.

"I want a pencil and paper, damn it," Dermot roared. "No, I don't want to make out my will. I want to write a poem."

Matt started laughing even though laughing really hurt his arm and the ground seemed to be getting less level every second. He wasn't aware of being led over to sit in the backseat of the car, but pretty soon that was what he was doing. After that, they drove him to the hospital.

IT WASN'T UNTIL he was being stitched up that something occurred to him.

The money was gone.

20

INSTEAD OF BEING MAD, JACK SEEMED IN A STATE OF shock.

Matt understood, or thought that he did. It wasn't every day that his father got married. It also wasn't every day that Matt almost got himself killed.

He told his father everything while they were waiting at the hospital. *Everything,* even Disneyland. In fact, for a while it seemed like he couldn't stop talking.

Daisy excused herself when he started explaining what happened because he hadn't yet given his official statement to the police. She said she was truly glad he was all right.

He told her that for somebody without maternal instincts, she was truly great. She'd saved his life. Maybe a mother who stayed home and baked cookies could have done the same thing, but Daisy had really been something to see in her white wedding gown holding the big guy at gunpoint.

"Like a lioness with her cub," Jack said as she left.

Step-cub. That was okay, too.

NOW HE'D SETTLED down some. Except for the flesh wound in his arm, he felt almost normal.

It was after eleven when they arrived at the police station, because the hospital took a while deciding whether he should be released or kept overnight. He'd overheard two nurses talking. Dermot had some bad burns and broken ribs, plus his gunshot wound, but he'd be all right.

"Where's Lewis?" Matt asked the sergeant as they sat at a table in a small green room at the police station. Jack was beside him, still wearing his tux. He'd called a lawyer from the hospital, so the room was really crowded.

Everybody kept glancing at Matt, then looking away again.

At the table, the gray-haired lawyer looked like he'd been asleep when Jack phoned him. Rumpled.

Matt had caught a glimpse of himself before he left the emergency room. A walking scarecrow wasn't anyone to call another person rumpled.

"Lewis Rannulf is waiting for his father to arrive," the lawyer explained. "You're going to give the police your statement now, tell them what happened." He set a long yellow pad of paper on the table before him.

Everybody seemed to be waiting.

"Now?" Matt asked.

The lawyer nodded.

"We didn't do anything wrong," the boy began. "Honest. Neither did Dermot. He just worked for us."

"Perhaps," the sergeant suggested, "you should begin at the beginning."

As Mr. Rannulf came into the police station, he spotted his son standing near the water cooler. "Well," he said gruffly, "this is the last place I ever expected to find you."

Lewis barely glanced at him. "Did you bring my glasses?"

"Oh, yeah." The man reached into his shirt and handed him his old glasses with the taped frames. "What happened to the other ones?"

"They broke."

"It must've been one hell of a wedding. You're going to have to tell me what happened because the policeman who called didn't make a whole lot of sense." His father sat down and motioned to the next chair.

Lewis remained standing.

"Suit yourself." He waited. "So, what was it? Did Matt get you in trouble, or was it the old man?"

His glasses were smudged. Lewis held them out and breathed on them.

"Your eyes look different," Mr. Rannulf said uneasily. "Old. Not older. Old." He shrugged. "I don't usually see you without glasses. Sure, that must be it."

Lewis was about to wipe the fogged lenses on his shirt except that he couldn't seem to find an area that was clean.

"You're a mess. Here, take this." His father held out a handkerchief. "Your mother's a great one for clean hankies. I guess you lost the one she gave you."

"It got used to make a bomb." One of his father's eyebrows went up. "I blew up two cars tonight. And money. I blew up a lot of money, too." He sat, but not in the chair next to his father. "Three hundred—" He couldn't remember the exact sum remaining anymore, although before everything happened he had known right down to the last penny. "Something like $370,000."

"What in hell were you serving kids at that party?" his father barked suddenly.

Daisy stood near the window at the other side of the room, wearing slacks and a shirt. "Mr. Rannulf," she said, "I'd suggest that you listen very carefully to what your son has to say. I'm going for a short walk. I believe that Fred can come up with cups of tea if you'd like some."

The door closed behind her. "Your mother would say that," Mr. Rannulf said. "Tea." He walked up to the counter and spoke to the man sitting at a desk. "Is there any chance of me and the boy getting some tea here?"

The man nodded and went into an adjoining room to plug in a kettle.

"We'll want plenty of sugar." Mr. Rannulf returned, muttering that he would need more than tea to swallow what he was hearing. "Okay," he said. "You talk, I'll listen."

THE POLICE READ Matt his rights, just like he had seen on TV.

Like they did with criminals.

As he gave his statement and the two men made notes, he had the weird feeling that he was talking about someone else. Like he was giving a book report. Not that there was any real chance of confusion. His arm hurt enough to remind him that everything was true.

"What's going to happen to us?" Matt asked the lawyer after he signed his statement and the sergeant left the room.

"That depends on the charges that are brought. You might end up with six months' probation."

Jack groaned.

"But we didn't—"

"I know. You've said several times that you believe you did nothing wrong. However, the authorities may be inclined to view your actions as possession of stolen property." He put his papers into a narrow briefcase and snapped it shut. "I'll have a few words with your father now. Perhaps you can wait outside."

"Can I ask a question?"

The man straightened. "Sure."

"What about Dermot?"

"He's an adult. He could be seen as taking advantage of two innocent young boys, leading you astray."

"It wasn't that way. If anybody got led astray, we led him. Ask Lewis."

"Matt," the lawyer said, "the charges aren't up to me. This is only a guess, but if he has no prior record he may get off with probation. Say, two years."

"What about the stuff we bought? What happens to it?"

"Matt," Jack said stiffly, "right now you have a lot more to be concerned about than—"

"No," the man said, "it's a fair question. Probably the merchandise will be sold at auction and the proceeds turned over to the government."

That's what he was afraid of. Lewis wouldn't get his computer and his glasses were broken. They were back where they started. "Will Dermot's poetry books be sold, too?"

The lawyer cleared his throat. "The books wouldn't be worth much unsold." He paused. "Are you asking whether he's going to end up giving poetry readings?"

Matt nodded.

As the lawyer turned away, Matt caught the ghost of a smile. "I suppose that's not impossible."

———————

DAISY CAME UP to him when he returned to the waiting area. Lewis and his father were sitting in chairs at the other side of the room. Matt was positive that Lewis knew he was there, but the other boy didn't even look up.

Jack came out. "We can leave," he said to Daisy. "The matter isn't over." He frowned at Matt. "Not by far."

"My arm hurts," Matt said, and not just because it did. "A whole lot."

"You've been shot, and you're too old to spank—" Jack's voice rose.

Daisy laid her hand on his arm. "Perhaps we should all go home now and try to get some sleep. This matter won't go away before morning."

Reluctantly, her new husband agreed.

"YOU CAN'T TOUCH him," Mr. Rannulf growled at the sergeant. "The boy is a minor."

"Oh," the sergeant said, "we can touch him, all right."

"Can you tell me that, at his age, you wouldn't have done the same thing? He's thirteen!"

Lewis felt unreal as he signed his statement. Empty. When he was in the ditch, positive that he was about to be killed, a vacant feeling had come over him.

He didn't know what he used to be filled with, only that it wasn't there anymore.

"YOUR MOTHER IS going to fuss," Lewis' father said as they walked out to the truck. "You know that. She might even take up praying again." He hesitated. "Crank the window open all the way before you get in."

Lewis couldn't smell himself anymore. He nodded.

"You'll take a shower when you get home." He turned the key in the ignition but made no move to pull out. "There's only one thing I want to know. If you were so eager to turn over all that money to an old drunk, why didn't you think of me?"

"We weren't going to tell any adults." They'd hired Dermot. He wasn't like a parent, or a teacher, or a friend. At least, not at first.

Mr. Rannulf grunted. "In your shoes, I probably wouldn't have done any different." He pulled out. "So it's all gone? Every cent?"

"It all blew up."

"I heard something at the police station about the Potts dump being cordoned off." He chuckled. "Thanks to you and Matt, everybody in town has to keep their garbage at home until the police finish sifting through the rubble."

CHAPTER
21

LEWIS DIDN'T REMEMBER MUCH AFTER HE GOT HOME, except that his mother started crying as soon as he came through the door.

At first it looked like she was going to hit him, and then she didn't.

It wouldn't have been a good idea for her to hit him.

Nobody was ever going to hit him again.

His father orderd Lewis into the shower. As Lewis shut the bathroom door, he could hear his parents both talking rapidly in low voices.

Usually they yelled.

WHEN HE WAS clean, he came out in his pajamas and asked for bandages for his feet. His mother took a look at the raw blisters left from running in his band shoes, and she started to cry again. His father handed him the box of Band-Aids, then told him to go to bed.

The last Lewis saw, they were both sitting at the kitchen table. Both stared straight forward.

———————

HE WAS SLEEPING so deeply that he didn't hear Corinne come in with the baby and put him in his crib.

The crib and the bed were close enough that sometimes when Joey woke up at night, Lewis reached through the bars and held his hand. That always shut him up so they both could get some sleep.

Sometimes he talked to him.

Read stories that the baby was too young to understand.

Sang lullabies nobody else would ever hear.

He didn't even realize that Joey was there until some time during the night, when he half woke up or maybe quarter woke up. He was holding the baby's hand.

Or maybe Joey was holding his. The baby was asleep, but Lewis kept on lying there with Joey's tiny fingers wrapped around one of his.

He listened to the baby's even breathing, listened and listened.

Filled himself with it.

Slept again.

HE AWOKE AT dawn to the sound of Joey giggling for no reason. "What?"

Joey kicked out against his headboard. "Money."

"Money's all gone," Lewis murmured and turned over. His kneecaps ached. His eyelids ached. He ached all over. He needed to sleep for a million years, but Joey was struggling to his feet. Lewis put his pillow over his head. "Go back to sleep. It's too early."

Corinne came into the room in her cotton robe. She leaned over the crib and picked up her son. "Hi, little guy." She turned to Lewis. "Mom and Dad said you had some excitement last night."

They could say that, all right.

"I was at a party." She sat at the foot of Lewis' bed. "We had so much fun, and we got in really late." She made a face at Joey. "We did, didn't we? Really late." She turned back to Lewis. "Mom and Dad were just going to bed when I came in the door. They both looked wiped out, and they said it had something to do with you. So, was the wedding party fun?"

She didn't know. He pulled his sheet up higher. "I'll tell you later."

"Somebody needs changing." She laid the baby back in his crib and reached for a diaper. "Oh, Lew. You phoned last night about that old crib mattress. I remembered afterward. Mom put it out in the street for the trash collector, but a man came along in a pickup. He asked if he could take it for his Saint Bernard pup."

"No," Lewis moaned.

"I said it was okay. Well, why not?" Again, she leaned toward the baby. "Why not, right? Why not let him have it?"

"Money," Joey gurgled.

As SOON AS his sister headed out of the room, Lewis slipped out of bed and got dressed. Corinne would find out what happened as soon as their parents woke up.

Matt. He had to call Matt.

There was one good thing about Matt sleeping on the sofabed in the den. He had a phone directly next to him.

Lewis waited until the shower was running, then he went out into the hall and dialed.

"Hello?" It was Matt's grandmother. She sounded sleepy.

"Uh . . . Mrs. Snow?"

"Yes?"

"It's Lewis Rannulf. Can I speak to Matt, please?"

Immediately a tone of disapproval came into her voice. "He's asleep upstairs in his own room."

There was a click as another phone was picked up. "Hello?" Jack said in a groggy voice.

Matt's dad was supposed to be on a boat, on his honeymoon.

"Who is it?" Daisy asked in the background.

They must have decided to stay in Potts because of what had happened the night before.

He should have figured that they would.

"Go back to sleep," Mrs. Snow said. "I'll take care of it." One phone clicked down. "When Matt wakes up, I'll tell him that you phoned."

Click. She hung up on him.

No! He had to talk to Matt now.

Remembering something, Lewis dug into his bureau drawer.

HIS BIKE WAS still at Dermot's. After locating a pair of rubber thongs, he headed out on foot.

There was only one Saint Bernard pup in town. All the kids knew where it lived because it was so cute. Alfredo.

Lewis made a slight detour that would take him past the small white house where Alfredo's owner lived.

HE STOOD OUTSIDE the chain-link fence with the sign reading BEWARE OF THE DOG. Sure enough, lying on the front porch to one side of the welcome mat was a definitely turquoise, definitely thick, definitely taped-up crib mattress. Beside it lay a blue dog bowl.

Bounding around the side of the house came the pup himself, a regular fuzzball. He was not a dog anyone needed to beware of.

"Werf," said Alfredo, poking his nose through the chain-link fence.

Lewis reached over to pet him. "You don't want it," he said. "Trust me."

HE STOOD IN the yard below Matt's room and pressed the CALL button on his walkie-talkie. Matt kept his unit in his bedside table, so he should be able to hear the sound.

Again, Lewis pressed it.

Again.

He was about to hurl the walkie-talkie through the upstairs window out of frustration when Matt finally answered. "What? What? What time is it?"

"Seven." Lewis kept his mouth right against the unit so he wouldn't have to speak loudly. "How are you feeling?"

He thought the sound was a laugh. "I don't want to know."

"Matt? It's alive. It's back." Briefly he told him about Corinne and the man with the dog. "What do you want me to do with the money?"

Matt didn't hesitate. "Drive a stake through its heart."

That was okay then.

At the side of the house, Lewis found green garbage bags full of paper plates and streamers from the wedding reception, plus some empty bags. He took two.

ALFREDO SAT NEXT to him, wagging his tail, as Lewis ripped a strip of tape from the bottom of the mattress. He reached deep inside and removed the plastic sacks.

Alfredo sniffed them. So did Lewis. Okay, maybe they smelled a little like Joey's diapers. Lewis had smelled a lot worse at the dump.

He put the money into one of the bags, put a second bag over it just in case the first one tore, then walked out again, shutting the gate carefully behind him.

"WHAT DO YOU have in the bag?" the minibus driver asked as he got on and deposited his coins.

Lewis told her.

The woman laughed. "Don't you wish it was? Let me guess. That's your laundry."

He went back and took a seat.

WHEN HE GOT off the bus in Upper Potts, the bottoms of his feet felt numb and one of his bandages had worked loose.

He limped the block to the police station where he'd been the night before. Several people were already at work as he walked through the door with his bundle. He didn't recognize any of them, although he supposed Matt would. He went up to the counter and set the bag on the floor.

A uniformed woman stood up from a computer terminal. She walked over. "Hi."

"Hi," Lewis said.

"What can I do for you today?"

"I found something. On the beach trail. I found it a while ago, but I'm turning it in now." He lifted the bag slightly so she could see it, then set it down again.

"And what is it that you found?"

He was trying to figure out the answer to that question.

People had been willing to kill him for what he had found.

He'd busted his butt for it, twisted himself all out of shape, driven everything else from his life, put his family in danger. What was it really?

He could play games with what was inside that bag, spend it on great stuff, use it to go places, open new worlds.

Close them.

The woman was waiting. "You found . . ."

Lewis reached into the bag and took out one of the plastic sacks. He set it on the counter.

Her eyes widened.

"It's just money," the boy said.

ABOUT THE AUTHOR

E. M. GOLDMAN lives in a small town in British Columbia where nothing ever happens. She is the author of the young-adult novel *Detective 10th Grade* and the play *The Perils of Cinderella; or, The Vampire's Bride,* as well as numerous science fiction and fantasy short stories.